The Cunning Cruise Ship Caper
A Sandy Fairfax Teen Idol Mystery
Book 3

by

Sally Carpenter

For information, email Cozy Cat Press, cozycatpress@aol.com or visit our website at: www.cozycatpress.com

COZY CAT
P R E S S

ISBN: 1 9398165 21
Printed in the United States of America
Cover design by Paula Ellenberger
www.paulaellenberger.com

10 9 8 7 6 5 4 3 2 1

Acknowledgements

It seems inevitable that every cozy mystery series includes a story set aboard a cruise ship. And why not? Exotic locations, great weather, interesting passengers, an exciting getaway—and murder. The idea for this book came from a cruise I took in 1999, a specialty trip planned for Monkees fans. About fifty fans traveled on the Carnival Ecstasy along with the regular guests for a weekend jaunt to Nassau. Special activities were set up just for our group—a cocktail party, a concert by one of the Monkees, and a Halloween costume gala. All of us had a great time and no murders took place. I used many of my experiences from that event in this book, including having my hair braided in Nassau. I had fun recalling those vacation memories and my hope is that the reader will enjoy an entertaining "cruise" as well.

I'd like to thank my extraordinary publisher, Patricia Rockwell; the other authors with Cozy Cat Press; Timm Sinclair for the book cover concept, and the sisters and misters of Sisters in Crime, especially the Los Angeles chapter.

LOS ANGELES 1993
Chapter 1: Little Sister

It was bad enough that I unwittingly got my sister involved in a murder investigation; but first I had to lie just to get past her front door. I stood on the porch of her tiny rented bungalow, tucked away on a congested side street in the not-so-affluent part of Canoga Park. The din of cars driving by and kids yelling filled the air. Some of the nearby houses sported peeling paint and yards filled with trash and brown grass. A couple of stray dogs roamed the cracked sidewalk. Some unsavory-looking teenagers hung out on the corner, their faces seeming to challenge anyone walking by. The neighborhood had deteriorated since I'd last visited some years ago. Just goes to show how out of touch I was with my family. I pressed the intercom button beside the front door of my sister's house.

"What if she says no?" My agent, Marshall Ellis, was such a pessimist.

"That's why I brought you along, Marshall. If anyone can talk my sister into doing something, you're the man. You could charm a parka off an Eskimo. You talked me into appearing on that dreadful sitcom last week, didn't you?"

"I'm sure you don't appreciate all the exposure that guest spot landed you."

"Yeah, and I almost landed in the morgue, thanks to a friendly neighborhood killer."

"All I did was secure the role for you. I never told you to snoop around into something that was none of your business."

Marshall took a silk handkerchief out of the breast pocket of his Brooks Brothers suit and blew his nose. An autumn breeze—or what passed as fall in Southern California—stirred up dust and pollen that made his allergies kick in. He repocketed his hanky. I was more leisurely clad in a polo shirt and jeans, not that my sister would notice.

"Honestly, Ernest, you take the prize as my most difficult client."

"Thank you. It's nice to know I'm an expert in something."

A female voice crackled over the wall speaker. "Who is it?"

I hoped that the cheap audio system would distort my voice. "It's your brother."

"Warren?"

I made my voice a little deeper that normal. "Yeah, that's right."

Marshall Ellis, my agent and mother hen, started to speak. I motioned for him to keep quiet. I didn't need him blowing my cover.

"But you usually call first," she said.

That sounded like something my ingratiating brother would do. "I was in the neighborhood and thought I'd drop by."

A pause. "Give me a minute."

The intercom clicked off. I exhaled in relief.

Marshall shot me a look. "Celeste won't be happy when she finds out you tricked her."

"That's the only way she'll let me inside. Either that or I kick the door in."

"I'll wait in the car. I'm not getting involved in your family fights."

From the other side of the door I heard footsteps. "Stay

here, Marshall. If my sister kills me, I'll need you as an eyewitness."

First came the sound of locks unlatching and then the door opened. My sister, the baby of the family, still looked like a doll at age thirty-three (five years younger than myself), despite the threadbare blouse and slacks she wore. She was pretty, not in a fashion model sense but in a girl-next-door way. Her straight blond hair was pulled back in a ponytail, much the same way I wore my long hair. When it came to looks, my family was blessed with good genes; brother Warren was ruggedly handsome, and I had ended up as the cute teen idol pin-up boy.

"I'm glad you stopped by," she said. "I just finished making some coffee cake."

I stepped inside so she couldn't slam the door in my face. I spoke in my natural voice. "Hi, Sis. It's good to see you. You look great."

She looked confused and angry. "That sounds like Ernest."

"Yeah, it's me."

"You didn't tell me Ernest was with you."

"Warren isn't here. That was me on the intercom. I'm sorry, but I thought you might not want to see me."

Her lips went into a tight line, and she clenched her fists. "You never stop, do you? You used to pull that trick on me all the time, pretending you were Warren. You haven't changed a bit."

"Sis, please, will you at least listen to me? I have something important to ask you."

"I don't want to do anything for you."

Marshall came inside, his leather shoes hitting the hardwood floor with quick thuds. "You should hear him out, Miss Farmington."

"Who's that?" Celeste raised her voice. "How many people did you bring here?"

"It's all right. He's okay. It's Marshall Ellis, my agent. He's the only other person here."

My agent leaned in and took my sister's hand in a firm shake. "Hello, Miss Farmington. It's a pleasure to meet you. Ernest has told me so much about you. I've enjoyed listening to your records from the '70s."

"Oh. Those old things."

I said, "Look, Sis, I want to patch things up between us. Just give me five minutes, that's all. Then if you still say no, I'll leave. Please?"

"Miss Farmington, Ernest has a good job offer that would benefit you a great deal. I'd recommend that you at least give him a chance."

Her shoulders sagged as she let out a sigh, but her face still looked hard. "All right, Ernest. Come in and let me have a look at you."

I stepped up to Celeste, took her hands, and placed them on my face—that's how a blind person "sees." I closed my big baby blue eyes as she ran her digits across my features.

"You shaved off your beard."

"It was itchy." Truth was, Marshall made me whack off my overgrown whiskers recently when I set out on my first public appearance in years.

She patted my pudgy cheeks. "Have you gained weight?"

"A little." I'd been out of work for so long I'd let myself go flabby.

"May we sit down?" Marshall asked.

"Oh. Yes," she said. "There's the sofa." She gestured toward a worn, tan-upholstered couch in the middle of the sparsely decorated room.

He sat on the sofa. "I heard you say something about fresh coffee cake. May we have some?"

I glared at him. My sister said, "Sure, I suppose so. I'll go get it."

"Can I help you, Sis?"

"No. I can manage—like I have for years." With that she left, striding with confidence along a well-memorized and unobstructed path across the bare tile floor and into the kitchen.

As soon as she was out of view, I sat beside Marshall and whispered, "You really take the cake. Soon as you come in, you're feeding your face."

"I know what I'm doing," he said in a low voice. "People relax when they're eating. If you sister is noshing on comfort food, she'll be more receptive to what you have to say."

"So that's why you're always eating when you're at my house. You're manipulating me into doing something for you."

"It works, doesn't it?"

"I should warn you that my sister isn't used to having visitors, so she's lacking a bit in the social graces."

"Apparently that runs in the family."

Good thing I liked my agent or I'd have been offended.

Marshall pointed to the small TV set on a metal stand in one corner. "Your sister watches TV?"

"Mostly the news and concerts on PBS. She likes old movies, you know, musicals and the ones with lots of dialogue. And before you ask, she made those." I was referring to the small abstract clay sculptures that filled the otherwise empty built-in bookshelves.

"She did? That's amazing."

"She does it by feel. She's sold a number of her works, although I think most people buy them for the novelty of having something made by a blind girl."

Celeste returned with two small plates holding slices of still-warm coffeecake and two forks. I stood and took the plates.

"I'll serve this to Marshall," I said.

"Did you take my piece as well?" she asked.

"I thought this was for me."

"I didn't know you wanted any. I'll have to go back and get another—"

"No, here, you have it." Anything to keep her happy. I put the second plate and fork back in her hand. "I wasn't hungry." Now that was a lie. The cake smelled delicious. The food reminded me that all I had had for breakfast was a cup of coffee and a bowl of sugar-frosted cereal in milk.

"I suppose you want a beer," she said.

"I don't drink any more."

"Since when?"

"It's true, Miss Farmington," Marshall said. "He's been sober since shortly before Labor Day. I can vouch for that."

"That's a surprise. All right, then." She sat on a tattered upholstered chair facing the couch and took a bite of her snack. I resumed my seat. We made small talk about her latest ceramics show—along with a barb about my absence at the artist's reception—and the gang bangers living on her street. I regretted not asking for some coffee cake, as it looked fantastic.

I noticed an empty spot in the room. "What happened to your piano?"

"The only way I could make any money from it was to sell it."

Either Celeste was in desperate financial straits, or she'd given up on music forever.

Marshall said, "This coffee cake is delicious, Miss Farmington. Very moist."

"Thanks. I was trying out a new recipe."

After Celeste set her empty plate on the coffee table, Marshal said, "Are we ready to discuss the business at hand?"

"All right. Ernest, what was it you wanted?"

"Well, Sis." I rubbed my hands together. "Marshall, why

don't you tell her?"

My agent set his plate and fork on the coffee table and straightened his tie as he shifted into his negotiating mode. I eyed his piece of coffee cake. Would he notice if I pilfered it while he talked?

"Miss Farmington, your brother has an offer to perform on a cruise ship, a five-day trip with stops in Key West and Nassau. Two sixty-minute shows per night for four nights in an intimate lounge."

"I thought I was on for five nights," I said.

"The last night at sea is a Halloween costume gala. I told the organizers you were not interested in providing background music for parties." Marshall returned his attention to Celeste. "As I was saying, Miss Farmington, the organizers want another singer to perform with your brother."

"They don't think the mighty Sandy Fairfax can pull off a show all by himself?"

Sandy Fairfax was the *nom de plume* given to me by my former manager in 1974, and also the source of much friction among my relatives who never understood why my given name wasn't good enough for the public.

To save face, I said, "Most of my songs had backing vocals, so for the concerts they'll sound better with another voice." Truth is, I never knew who sang on my albums. The SuperTonic label hired anonymous session singers to provide the backing tracks after I recorded the leads.

"So you want me along just to prop you up?" she countered.

"No, no. You can do a solo or two if you want."

"A song or two? That's all?"

Marshall said, "Miss Farmington, you have to understand, these are short concerts. There simply won't be time for both you and Ernest to do a full set apiece."

"Why wasn't I asked to headline?"

Some questions have no right answers—this is one of them. Unfortunately, Marshall chose the honest answer.

"Because your brother is the bigger name."

"And whose fault is that?" Celeste stood, made a beeline for the living room window and crossed her arms. She wasn't looking out the window so much as turning her back on me.

I walked over, stood behind her, and lightly put my hands on her shoulders. "Look, one reason I'm here is so I can apologize. I realize that a long time ago I acted like a jerk. Maybe I should have done more for you at the time, but I was under contract and the studio had me on a tight leash."

"Baloney!" she said, or words to that effect. My sister doesn't swear often, but when she does, she's furious. "You could have pulled strings if you wanted to. You used to brag about how the studio pampered you and gave in to your demands."

"That was on my TV show. The record suits were another matter. SuperTonic wasn't so generous."

She returned to her chair. I sat back on the sofa and pushed the contrary cowlick out of my face.

"Sis, I can't get in a time machine and change history, but now it's 1993 and I'm offering you a chance to sing again. You can write some new songs for the show if you want. This gig will get your name out there again."

"Four nights on a cruise ship? Isn't that where oldies acts go when they can't fill stadiums or get airplay?"

"The money's good, Miss Farmington," said Marshall, the walking cash register. "You'll have first class accommodations and plenty of perks."

"C'mon, Sis, you need a vacation, get out of the house. See some new sights, have fun. You might even meet some of your old fans."

"I wasn't around long enough to have fans."

I got off the sofa and dropped to one knee beside her chair. "This would mean a lot to me personally. Remember how we used to sing together when we were kids? We made a great team. Why don't we make an effort to start over?"

"I don't know, Ernest." She rubbed her eyes. "I'm tired. Let me think about it."

"We don't have much time, Miss Farmington," said Marshall. "We need to sign the contracts right away. The cruise is only a few weeks away."

"Ernest, if I say no, will you still do the shows?"

Her reluctance was irritating me. "Are you going to say *no* just to keep me out of the limelight and so we can both be failures?"

Marshall gave an exaggerated cough. "Ernest and I need to be going. If you'll excuse us, Miss Farmington."

He stood, grabbed my shirt collar, and lifted me to my feet. I glared at him and opened my mouth to reply, but he held up his hand and gave me a look to stop me. Good thing my sister didn't see our exchange.

"Thanks again for the coffee cake," Marshall said. "Think about the offer and give me a call. I'll leave you my card." I shook my head at him—his cards didn't have Braille printing. "On second thought, would you remember my phone number if I tell you?"

"I can call Ernest."

"Please give us your answer by tonight. I hope you will say yes. I know you'll enjoy getting back on stage. We'll see ourselves out."

I gave Celeste a quick goodbye before Marshall pushed me out the door. On the sidewalk, we both put on our sunglasses against the bright SoCal sun.

Marshall couldn't wait to scold me. "What were you doing, antagonizing her like that? After that last crack, she wasn't going to listen to anything else we had to say."

"She was the one goading *me*."

"Sometimes, Ernest, you talk too much."

"She's going to say no just to spite me. I know it. If she can't have a comeback, she won't let me have one either."

"Come on, let's not argue here. I need to get back to the office and, besides, you've parked on a red curb. Ernest, you're lucky you didn't get a ticket."

"From the looks of this street, the police have more important things to deal with than parking tickets."

We hopped in my car, a 1964 poppy red Mustang convertible with bucket seats, spoke wheels and palomino interior. Street parking is impossible to find near my sister's house, so Marshall and I had carpooled from his Beverly Hills office. I had the top down and my side window rolled down. I'm left-handed, so I steered with my left hand and rested my right atop the gearshift knob. Traffic was sluggish on the 101 Freeway. Sitting among stalled cars wasn't helping my foul mood, so I hit the nearest off-ramp and sped the Mustang along the surface streets. Even with the top down, we didn't generate much of a breeze in the car. Just as well—Marshall hates when his dark curly locks get mussed up.

"I'll find you another girl," he offered. "I know some bright young singers you'd enjoy working with."

"I don't want another girl."

"What if Celeste says no?"

I kept my eyes on the road and frowned.

"What's the history behind you and your sister? What haven't you told me?"

"She accuses me of sabotaging her singing career so I could be the only celebrity in the family. She thinks I deliberately set out to wreck her."

"Did you?"

"Of course not! No, not intentionally. I don't know. Things were so crazy in those days. I could barely keep up with what I was doing, let along run herd on my sister's life as well. She's always been unpredictable. One minute she wants to do everything herself, and the next she's helpless."

"In that case, is it such a good idea to hire her? What if she folds up in the middle of a show?"

"Celeste is okay once she's in front of an audience. It's just that she has these habits that help her cope, so don't ask her to change her pattern. It's a bear trying to push her out of her comfort zone. If this gig works out, maybe she'll take responsibility for her future and stop expecting me to do it for her." I stopped at a red light and shifted into neutral.

"Did she have a bad manager? I've heard her records, and she had the talent to go far. She could have easily been one of the top folk rock stars of the '70s."

"You know how this business is, Marshall." The light turned green. I shifted and roared forward, passing the slowpoke ahead of me who was only going the speed limit. "A lot of talent gets squashed along the way. She begged me to get her on my TV show. For some reason, that fell through the cracks. She wanted to open for my concerts, so I asked my handlers. They said no, my audiences wouldn't appreciate her type of music. I didn't argue. Maybe I should have pushed harder. Maybe I could have done more to promote her. Maybe if I hadn't opened my big mouth to that reporter . . ."

"The one who quoted you as saying Celeste was a 'poor little crippled blind girl?'"

"Stupid tattler took it out of context. Back then I was always joking around, saying silly stuff I didn't think anyone took seriously. I don't remember exactly what I said at the time but I never meant . . . anyway, the idiot made me sound like a monster and, of course, Celeste heard about it. She's still sore about that."

When I reached a certain office building in Beverly

Hills, I pulled down a side street and into the parking lot in back. I took a ticket from the parking attendant in the booth, parked, and got out of the car.

Marshall closed his side door behind him. "Are you coming inside?" He sounded surprised.

"Yeah. I want to use your phone."

We rode the elevator to Marshall's third-floor office that he shared with other independent entertainment agents and managers. He stopped at his secretary's desk to pick up his messages while I went inside his office, perched atop his pretentious mahogany desk, picked up the receiver, and punched a number into the phone. I didn't have to wait long before someone answered.

"Hello, Farmington residence," said a heavily accented voice.

What was the name of my parents' maid? I'd only met her once. "Hi, Imelda, it's Ernest. Is my mother home?"

"Sí, one minute."

After a pause, a familiar voice came on the line. "Ernest, darling. I was just thinking about you. I'm so glad you called. How are you?"

"I'm fine, Mother."

Marshall stepped into the room, closed the door, and mouthed the words, "Your mother?" I motioned to him to shut up.

"Look, Mother, I have a favor to ask you."

Marshall pushed me off the desk and picked up the file folder I was sitting on. He occupied his oversized leather executive chair and fussed with some paperwork. I resumed my desktop seat.

"Mother, I have a new job. I'll be doing some concerts onboard a cruise ship to the Bahamas."

"How lovely. Your father and I loved our trips to Nassau. You'll have a wonderful time."

"The problem is, I want Celeste to perform with me and

she won't do it."

"That's a pity. Why not?"

"I don't know. You know how she gets in a snit sometimes. I really want her to come with me."

"I shouldn't be surprised. Celeste isn't comfortable in crowds or strange places."

"Mother, she needs to get out in the world. She's cooped up in that little house like a recluse. She needs to meet people and have fun. She's just shriveling away."

"I don't know, Ernest. It's hard for her to get around."

"I'll be there to help. I'll wait on her hand and foot. Mother, will you talk to Celeste and make her change her mind?"

Marshall snatched the phone receiver out of my hand and whispered, "Ernest, are you out of your mind?"

I grabbed the phone back and said to my mother, "I know she'll get a kick out of singing again."

"Celeste is quite happy with what she's doing. She hasn't said anything about performing again."

"She'd said nothing because she's scared."

"Really, Ernest, don't you think your sister's old enough to make up her own mind?"

I should have known mother would take Celeste's side. She always did. "Here, I want you to talk to my agent."

I shoved the receiver into Marshall's hand. First, he looked at the phone and then at me and sighed. For a moment I thought he would hang up. Then he put the receiver to his ear and adopted his best wheeling-dealing attitude.

"Hello, Mrs. Farmington, this is Marshall Ellis. I'm your son's agent. I believe this opportunity would help Celeste re-launch her singing career. It's a small venue, friendly audience, low-keyed atmosphere. During the day she'll have time to relax. We'll have a top band and put on a quality show that will make her proud." He listened for a moment and handed the receiver back to me. "She wants to talk to you."

I took the phone. "Mother, this gig means the world to me. I've always wanted to do a show with Celeste. Remember how we used to sing duets when we were kids? I know she'll enjoy it too. It'll be like the old times. Please, Mother?"

"All right, Ernest, I'll see what I can do. But you know how stubborn your sister can be."

That may be true, but whenever my mother made a request, we children always obliged. "Thanks, Mother. I owe you for this. Call me back soon as you talk to her, okay?"

"Of course, dear. Bye, now. Love you."

"Love you too, Mother." I hung up.

Marshall didn't even glance up from his paperwork. "Will you get off my desk?"

"Why, am I ruining the finish?"

He eyed me. "Shouldn't you go home in case your mother calls?"

"Okay, but I know you'll miss my company."

As I was halfway to the door, Marshall added. "Ernest, I have to give the cruise line an answer tonight. If your sister won't do the gig, they need to line up another act PDQ."

"Okay, okay. I'll let you know."

"Do you still want the shows without Celeste?"

"I don't know."

I didn't mean to slam the door on my way out. Marshall knows me well enough not to take my outbursts personally. I stopped at the secretary's desk long enough to validate my parking ticket and then headed to my home in the Hollywood Hills. I puttered around the house, hoping Celeste wouldn't force me to decide to do the shows without her. If she said no and I went on ahead, she'd once again claim I was trying to show her up. If I stayed home, my own sputtering career would sink even further. And if she joined me and screwed up the show . . .

The phone rang.

Chapter 2: Home Is Where The Heart Is

My mother called with the good news. She never told me what she said to Celeste to make her say yes, but I didn't want to jinx the deal by prying. I contacted Marshall, and he said if Celeste didn't have management, he'd be happy to represent her. Clever guy—he just wanted another potential moneymaker in his stable of clients. I didn't mind, because I knew he'd work hard to get us both the best deal. Then he started jabbering about putting a band together. I said, forget the musicians—what I really needed was a personal trainer. I wasn't going on stage looking like an overweight blob.

I dug out my address book and starting calling every session player and arranger I knew. Finding a band was harder than I'd imagined. I'd been out of touch for too long. Some of the best guys I'd worked with had moved on to other occupations. Others refused, scared off by my reputation as an irresponsible drunk. Marshall put out some feelers and came up with Frank Oswald, a young kid who was in diapers during my heyday. My agent assured me the guy was smart, talented, amiable and, most important of all, could probably put up with me.

I called Celeste and asked her to move in with me until we left for the cruise. "We've got a busy schedule ahead of us. I'll be driving you to rehearsals and who knows where else. Running out to Canoga Park each day would be out of my way."

"If it's such a bother, I can take the bus."

"From your place to Hollywood? How long would that

take?"

"I don't want to inconvenience you."

"It's no problem. I'll do the cooking. You can use the pool and the Jacuzzi. Think of it as a mini-vacation at your own private hotel. Besides, you're not in the best neighborhood. You'll be safer at my place."

"You don't like my house?" She sounded a bit indignant.

"I love your house. It's your street that worries me."

"I'm careful."

"I'm sure you are. Look, this will go more smoothly if you are here. It's just for a few weeks."

Celeste finally agreed to the move-in after I said I'd pay for her food. The next day, I drove out to pick her up. When I arrived, I discovered she was bringing more than just a suitcase; she had packed nearly all of her belongings, "just in case I need it," she explained. She had several boxes full of books-on-tape cassettes, a tape recorder, her entire wardrobe and her stuffed animals. She also wanted to bring her houseplants so they would stay watered. With a groan, I stuffed the Mustang, back seat and trunk, full of her things. While she filled a travel bag with her toiletries, I quietly went around the house and checked to make sure the windows and back door were secured, the lights turned out and the AC and faucets turned off. She wouldn't appreciate me playing big brother, but I didn't care. Criminals loved breaking into empty houses.

"Sis, did you put a hold on your mail? Did you tell a neighbor you were going so they could keep an eye on the place?"

"Everything's fine, Ernest. And stop nosing around. I already locked up everything."

Maybe she couldn't see, but she always knew what I was doing.

When we got to my house, I carried the boxes up the

stairs to the guest bedroom where she'd be staying. My bedroom was nearby, two doors down the hall if she needed something during the night. I took Celeste on a tour of the house. She hadn't visited for a long time, and I'd moved some of the furniture. She needed to walk through a new place a couple of times before she'd remembered the layout.

While she was upstairs unpacking, I dug out a business card someone had given me at my last job and made a phone call.

A perky, young female voice said, "Good afternoon, Dance Delight Studio, how may I help you?"

"Ah, is Cinnamon Lovett there?"

"I'm sorry; she's with a student now. If you're interest in signing up for classes, I can give you the information—"

"No, thanks. I don't want classes, but I need to speak with her right away. Can you take a message? Tell her Sandy Fairfax called. When's a good time for me to call back?" I rarely gave out my unlisted home number. For all I knew this receptionist could be a rabid fan and potential stalker.

"Just a minute; she just stepped in the office. Hold on."

After a few seconds of annoying hold music, the voice I longed to hear came on the line. "Hello, Sandy. How nice to hear from you. How are you?"

"Hi, Cinnamon, I'm fine." Actually, I was feverish. My heart thumped. I always felt a little goofy whenever I talked with her.

"What can I do for you?"

"Ah, I'm doing some shows and I need a choreographer. Are you available?"

"That's great! I'm so glad you're performing again. But I'm not sure I can squeeze you in. In a few weeks I'll be leaving on a cruise."

"Really? So am I. I'm doing a week of shows aboard the

SS Zodiac."

A pause. "Say that again."

"The SS Zodiac. Why? Is something wrong?"

"Five nights to Key West and Nassau?"

"Yeah, how do you know?"

"Sandy, that's the same trip I'm taking!"

Yes, there is a God! In his generosity he had placed the girl of my dreams on the cruise with me. My mind raced with vivid fantasies of Cinnamon and me on the deck together, sipping mocktails in the moonlight, sharing a sensuous meal by candlelight, slow dancing in the lounge with me muttering sweet nothings in her ear—

"My boyfriend is coming with me. Doesn't that sound romantic?"

Oh, God, why do you mock me? In my mind's eye, the ship's anchor crashed through the deck beside me, and I plunged into the briny sea.

"Boyfriend? I didn't know you were engaged."

"I'm not. I mean, we're not. He's an old friend I dated years ago and we're reconnecting."

"Oh."

"I need to run, Sandy. I have to set up for my next pupil. You said something about choreography?"

I forced my mind out of mourning and back into business mode. "Um, yes, if you could work with me on the show, that'd be great."

"I'd love to, Sandy, but we'll have to move fast. How soon can you get the music to me?"

Music? I hadn't even made up the set list. Then I heard a crash and a scream. I made a vague promise about meeting Cinnamon sometime tomorrow and gave her a hurried goodbye. I hung up the phone and rushed to the foot of the stairs where I found my sister sprawled on the floor.

"Are you all right?" I said.

"What did you leave on the step?"

Apparently, when I was taking the boxes upstairs, one of her shoes had fallen out. I'd just stepped around the object with the intention of picking it up later—my usual housekeeping routine. I'd forgotten that Celeste couldn't see obstacles. When we were growing up, the family rule was *always pick up after yourself so Celeste doesn't trip.*

I took her hands and pulled her up. "Did you hurt yourself?"

"No, I guess not."

"Sorry, I've been a bachelor for too long. Here, sit down."

I led her into a chair in the living room. After my wife left with the kids in 1988, my housekeeping skills eroded. I made a quick reconnaissance of the first floor rooms and picked up all the stray objects. I was going to scout out the second floor when Celeste said she was hungry. I went to the kitchen to scrounge up dinner and start plotting ways I could get Cinnamon away from her boyfriend. Out of habit, I turned on the kitchen TV as I cooked—a four-bedroom house can get lonely for a lone guy. I set out the plates and utensils on the large kitchen island where I usually ate. When Celeste entered the room I showed her where to sit, on one of the bar stools beside the island. We talked as I put together a feast of leftover meatloaf, mashed potatoes, veggies and Jell-O with fruit.

"So what do you want to watch while we eat?" I asked.

My sister does a good job watching TV; she can usually figure out what's going on from the dialogue, music and sound effects. When we went to the movies as kids, we'd sit in the back row away from the other patrons and I'd explain the action to her.

"What's on?"

I took the remote and started flipping through the channels.

"Wait, stop, back up," she said. "You passed it."

"What?"

"I thought I heard your show."

Sure enough, my claim to pop culture fame, that cheesy pseudo-spy series *Buddy Brave, Boy Sleuth*, had just started on Nickelodeon.

"You want to watch that?" As angry as she's been with me all these years, I assumed Celeste would have nothing to do with my work.

"Buddy makes me laugh. Besides, I like watching you squirm when the villains have you tied up." Every sibling's revenge fantasy.

We settled in with our food for the next sixty minutes while that underage undercover spy, Buddy Brave, chased the bad guys, aced his high school classes, romanced the girl guest star, spouted corny dialogue, and acted so wholesome he made the Hardy Boys look like rebels. Fortunately, Celeste was spared the sight of Buddy's late-1970s wardrobe of polyester plaids and paisley shirts, not to mention that horrific scarf that was knotted around my neck every week.

As fate would have it, today's episode was "The Scandalous Steam Ship Caper," featuring Buddy running around in the bowels of the engine room of a cruise liner. For the most part, I liked working on that episode because the cast and crew took a weekend cruise from Los Angeles to Mexico so we could film some of the scenes aboard a real ship. (This was the only time I'd ever taken a cruise. Although I've traveled the world, I was always in a hurry to get where I was going and so I flew).

Celeste enjoyed the show, often laughing in places that were not intentionally funny. "Do you think any of that is going to happen on our cruise?"

"Of course not. It's only a TV show."

"I hear you've turned into a real-life detective."

"I have not. I just got caught up in a couple of murder

cases, that's all."

"I never thought you'd do anything like that."

"Can I help it if people drop dead in front of me?"

"You were never any good at solving puzzles."

I was always miffed at the fact Celeste could put together jigsaw puzzles by feel faster than I could by sight. Sometimes I'd turn the pieces face down on the table just to make it harder for her.

"Fine," I said. "If any dead bodies turn up on the Zodiac, I'll let you figure it out."

Speaking of mysteries, on the TV the bad guys had Buddy tied up. The meanies tossed the kid over the ship's railing into the cold, dark sea just after he delivered his famous catch phrase, "Don't worry; I'll think of something!" For the underwater shots, the crew had built a replica of the ship's hull in the studio's water tank. And yes, the water was freezing—someone had forgotten to heat the water beforehand.

Buddy escaped by sticking his hands into the ship's moving propeller to cut the ropes off his bound wrists (how realistic is that?). We worked with the safety coordinator a long time on that scene so I could get the ropes off quickly and the studio wouldn't need to hire a new star for the show. On the TV, Buddy escaped his watery death trap (and showed up in the very next scene completely dry), saved the world, kissed the girl guest star, and got bawled out by his guardian for not cleaning his bedroom.

When we finished with both the show and dinner, I turned off the TV, stuck our dirty plates in the dishwasher, and took Celeste to my den. I showed her how to run the stereo and suggested she listen to some of my albums so she'd become familiar with the songs for the show.

"Do you have my records?" she asked.

"Of course."

"I haven't listened to them in years."

In the '70s, Celeste only managed to release two solo albums on a tiny obscure label rather than on a major force like SuperTonic. The label made no effort at promotion; her songs garnered minimal airplay and vanished. I dug out her vinyl from my collection.

"Do you know which one of your songs you want to do in the show?" I asked.

"No. I never had a big hit."

"Tell you what. I have to leave for a while. Why don't you listen to your records while I'm away and you can decide."

"You're leaving me alone?"

"Just for a couple of hours. I won't be away for long."

"Where are you going?"

"To my A.A. meeting."

"Oh, sure. I bet you're going to see a girlfriend."

I was annoyed. "I don't have a girlfriend. I told you I quit drinking. A.A. helps me cope. Do you want me stumbling around tipsy onboard the ship? I have to stay sober so I can look out for you. Look, I gotta run; I'm late as it is. If you need anything from the kitchen, help yourself. If the phone rings, let the answering machine pick up. Do you remember where the bathroom is?"

"Yes, big brother. I'm not an invalid."

I left her and dashed over to Beverly Hills for my weekly A.A. meeting. With the pressure of the upcoming shows and putting up with Celeste, I needed to stay dry in the worse way. On the way to the meeting, I wondered if having my sister in the show was such a good idea after all. So far our time together had been bumpier than this stretch of the freeway.

The meeting went well, but when I returned home, family matters got tense again. Celeste wanted a glass of brandy.

"I looked through your kitchen cabinets but didn't find

anything," she said.

"I don't have any alcohol in the house."

"I always have a brandy in the evening. It helps me relax."

"Sorry."

"I'd really like a brandy."

"I can't keep booze in the house. I don't trust myself. I'd end up drinking the bottle myself."

"You never had any willpower."

"Stop it. I'm tired and not in the mood for your attitude."

"I'll keep the bottle in my bedroom and lock the door so you can't get in."

"You think I don't have a key to every room in the house?"

"I'll call a locksmith and change the lock."

I sighed. "All right, if it means that much to you."

I backed the Mustang out of the garage for a trip to the all-night grocery store. I felt disgusted, buying alcohol right after an A.A. meeting. I stood in front of the liquor display, took a deep breath, and picked up a bottle. I'd been sober a couple of months; surely I could handle the thing without going off the deep end. I picked up some other items so the clerk wouldn't think I was a lush only interested in the booze. The clerk rang up the order and stuffed the bottle into a paper bag along with some groceries. I stuck the bag on the floor of the Mustang's back seat. At home, I put away the food and handed off the bottle to Celeste.

"Why don't you join me and we can talk?" she asked.

"No, I can't. Not to be rude, but I'm leaving the room now. I don't want to watch you drinking. I did too much of my boozing here in the house. Just turn out the lights when you go to bed. I've locked the doors and set the alarm. Good night and sleep well." I started for the stairs.

"Ernest?"

I stopped. "What?"

"Can I have a glass?"

I fetched a brandy glass from the kitchen and started to retire once again.

"Ernest?"

"What is it now?"

"What are you going to do on the cruise when all the other people are drinking?"

I hadn't thought of that. Cruise ships are filled with bars open all day and night with liquor available at almost every meal. My sobriety was going to take a beating once I hit the high seas.

Chapter 3: Am I Ready?

For the following weeks, I was too busy to think about drinking. On the first day of band rehearsal, I was awake far too early for a workout session at a gym with a personal trainer. I needed to lose weight so I wouldn't sink the ship. I also had to build up stamina for the high-energy concerts. After enduring the trainer's punishment, I dashed home for a quick shave and shower, tied my long blond hair back into my usual ponytail, and exchanged my workout gear for comfortable pants and shirts suitable for my dance session. For breakfast I made omelets. I piled Celeste's egg dish with veggies, cheese and ham, but had to forgo the cheese and meat for myself. My trainer forced me onto a strict diet that was going to slim me down by starvation. Since Celeste was going out in public, she put on a nice pantsuit. I drove the two of us to meet with our respective vocal coaches. Both of us needed some fine-tuning so we wouldn't lose our voices after the first show.

Next on the agenda was my dance lesson with Cinnamon at her studio in Northridge. I didn't have time to take Celeste back to the house, and she didn't want to wait in the car, so she tagged along. While I worked with Cinnamon, my sister sat on a bench along the wall of the studio, listening to the music and our conversation.

In the car afterwards, Celeste said, "She likes you."

"What? Who does?"

"That choreographer. She likes you."

"How would you know?"

"I heard it in her voice every time she talked to you."

"Cinnamon isn't fond of me. She has a boyfriend."

"When did that ever stop you?"

"What makes you think I like her?'

"Don't be silly, Ernest. You were gushing all over her. I was surprised you didn't ravish her on the spot."

"I'm too much of gentleman for that."

She replied with a loud, long laugh.

We stopped at Hamburger Hamlet in Sherman Oaks for a quick lunch before our rehearsal with the band. I insisted on a booth in the back for privacy, but not because I was concerned about getting accosted; many celebrities ate here. Rather, Celeste touched her food as she ate, and some people found that disgusting. Having grown up with her, my sister's habits didn't bother me. When the waiter came to take our order, I moaned. Due to my malnourishment diet, I couldn't order one of the delicious cheeseburgers that I loved. I was forced to make do with a salad and coffee. I looked out the window so I wouldn't have to watch my skinny sister enjoying a turkey sandwich with fries and a root beer float. That girl could eat a Porterhouse steak dinner with all the trimmings and never gain an ounce.

We didn't have time for talk since we were both busy chewing away, so I thought about what Celeste had said. Did Cinnamon pick up on my feelings about her? If so, she never showed it. During our time together she was thoroughly professional and efficient. Cinnamon was polite, but not overly friendly. We didn't talk about personal matters. Would I be able to make small talk with her once we were onboard, or would she be glued to this guy, whoever he was?

After we finished eating and I paid the tip and bill, we headed for a rented rehearsal studio on Sunset Boulevard— a smaller and less expensive facility than when I recorded my 1970s albums in the Capital Records building in

Hollywood.

It's a shame that the band practice didn't go as well as my dance lesson.

Frank had assembled some young, hungry musicians who appeared eager to please. I had told him I wanted clean-cut guys—no tattoos or outlandish hair—to compliment my teen idol image. No show-offs either—I was the star of the show. Frank was playing lead guitar as well as arranging the music, leading the band, and putting the show together. Besides him, we had the usual lineup of drums, rhythm guitar, bass and a three-man horn section—'70s music was heavy with the brass. I never played an instrument in my solo shows because I was too busy interacting with the audience. Celeste would handle keyboards. She was a good pianist, almost on par with my superior-in-every-way brother, a professional organist.

Frank introduced me to the other musicians. I showed Celeste the Yamaha keyboard that she'd be playing. She sat on the bench, placed her purse on the floor, turned on the instrument, and limbered up with some scales. She ran her fingers over her sheet music—Frank had found some of my songs transcribed into Braille music notation, which Celeste could read. The band and I ran through the songs on Frank's proposed set list. I was used to playing large arena shows and Frank said I'd have to tone down my energy and projection for the smaller venue. Unlike my big, rowdy concerts, this time I'm be doing more ballads and slow numbers—a cruise ship audience isn't likely to get up and dance. As we practiced, I thought the band members sounded pretty good—except for the keyboardist.

Celeste used to be a quick study—she'd hear a melody once and then play it through. But today she hit the wrong notes, forgot the lyrics, and played out of synch with the guys.

Frank pulled me aside. "I don't think Celeste is ready for

this."

"No, give her a little more time. It's only the first day."

Of course, I was biased—and stupid. If any of the other musicians had played that badly, I'd have booted them out on the street. We kept going, but Celeste didn't improve. The guys exchanged looks with each sour note she hit. Frank made some tactful suggestions to Celeste, which didn't help. Finally, in the middle of a song, she folded her arms atop the Yamaha, laid down her head, and cried.

Frank spoke loud enough for everyone to hear. "I'll get a replacement for tomorrow."

"Let me talk to her," I said.

"I know how you feel, Sandy, but we can't afford nervous breakdowns in the middle of the show."

"Give us a few minutes alone."

I told the band to take a break. After the others had cleared the studio, I closed the door, pulled a chair beside Celeste, and sat down. "Sis, it's Ernest. We're alone. Everyone else has left the room."

She raised her head and wiped her eyes with her fingers. "I can't do this. I'm not that good."

I handed her my handkerchief. "Don't say that. You used to be fantastic."

"That was a long time ago."

"You're just out of practice."

"I don't want to do this. I want to go home."

"You're giving up? I worked my butt off to get you onboard with this gig, and now you're making me look like an idiot."

"It's always about you, isn't it? All about what Sandy Fairfax wants. You don't care about what I want."

"I thought putting on a show was what you wanted."

"So did I," she said softly.

My patience was wearing out faster than my old tee shirts. "Look, Sis, if you want to bail out now, do it.

Marshall can break your contract. If you're not up to this, I'll take you home, and you can go back to your little clay statues and watching TV and reading books. But if you leave now, I never want to hear you complain about the past or blame me for missed opportunities or regret never going back on stage. I guess I was right in not helping with your singing career. You could have never pulled it off."

"Yes, I could!"

"So prove it!"

Celeste sat for a moment in silence. She fell into these quiet moods when she was thinking things over. "I'm not used to working with other people. I always played solo. I need to practice by myself. I can't jump into a rehearsal if I don't know the music."

"Okay, here's what we'll do. Tonight we'll go home and go over the songs. I won't bring you back to the studio until you're prepared. How does that sound?"

"That sounds good."

"Take as long as you want as long, as you're ready by tomorrow."

She smiled and punched me in the arm.

I rubbed the target. My baby sister can pack a wallop. "That hurt!"

"You really think I can do this?"

"I know you can."

She turned off the keyboard and picked up her purse. I helped her find a chair in the corner of the room. Then I went into the hallway to talk with Frank. He was hanging up the pay phone on the wall.

He said, "I just called a friend of mine. She'll be joining us for rehearsal tomorrow."

"That won't be necessary."

"Sandy, we can't afford to waste time on amateurs."

"Celeste will work out."

I prayed I was right. The last thing I needed was a room

full of guys furious at me for making a decision with my heart instead of my head (which is the usual way I ran my life). The band and I finished rehearsing without the keyboards. I hoped Celeste was listening so she'd learn the songs, but she was probably daydreaming.

I wrapped things up around seven o'clock. After the others left, Frank stuck around to work with me on the patter, stories and corny jokes that I would use between the songs—and you thought my witty remarks were off the cuff. A teen idol show is half music, half talk—the focus is on engaging the audience more than just playing tunes. Celeste offered some good suggestions for our onstage "sibling banter," most of which had me as the butt of the joke in the classic style of Donny and Marie. I think the reason she changed her mind about doing the gig was so she could pick on me in public.

We finally called it a day. Celeste looked tired, and I was fading fast. On the way home, I stopped at Gelson's grocery store to get Celeste's favorite foods and to purchase some low-calorie items for myself. I had run out of my standard soft drink, Mountain Dew, but this time I had to buy the *diet* version. Oh, the humanity. I was truly suffering for my art.

After I parked the Mustang in the garage, I unloaded and put away the groceries. Celeste offered to cook dinner. She's actually pretty handy in her kitchen where every single item was in place and the oven knobs were marked with ridges for the various settings. I showed her around my kitchen.

Her critique of my abode was, "It's disorganized. Don't you have a system for putting things away?"

"Yeah. Things go in the first available empty spot."

"Why don't you get the pans and food that I need and put them on the island? Otherwise, I'll be searching through the cabinets all night."

I prepared the kitchen for her and turned on the oven. While she cooked, I dug out an old electronic keyboard stashed away in my home recording studio. I didn't use it much because my instrument of choice is the guitar. I set up the keyboard in the living room, along with a tape player and cassettes of my songs. Frank's musical arrangements closely matched the records because that's what the fans wanted to hear—leave the long concert jams and endless guitar and drum solos to the FM radio crowd.

Celeste didn't like sitting on the kitchen stools, so we ate in the dining room. In deference to my diet, she made some surprisingly good fish fillets with a cauliflower, broccoli and mushroom side (surprising not because she made it, but because I'm not crazy about fish). She was miffed because we'd arrived home too late to watch *Buddy Brave*. I promised to set my VCR tomorrow to record the program (You'd think that I'd have a collection of the episodes, but the studio never gave me copies of the show).

I also told her to eat all snacks and desserts in the house so I wouldn't cheat on my diet. Giving up tasty food as well as booze—how would I survive? As soon as I returned from this cruise, I'd be hitting the Baskin Robbins store for a triple-scoop banana split sundae.

After dinner, I cleaned up the kitchen while Celeste practiced. She attacked the keyboard as if she had a personal vendetta against it. I offered to help, but she insisted she'd learn better on her own. Celeste could be strong-minded when she wanted to prove something. While she played, I camped out in the den to mellow out with some TV. When I was ready to turn in, I checked on Celeste. She was still playing, her face a mask of determination.

"Why don't you take a break?" I asked.

"What?" I'd startled her.

"Are you still working on that?"

"You said I had to learn this by tomorrow."

"I was kidding."

"I'm not."

"Do you want your brandy now?"

"I'm not ready for bed."

"I was going to share a drink with you."

"You said you didn't drink."

"I meant brandy for you; O'Doul's for me."

"I don't have time."

She started to play again. I grabbed her hands.

"You need to rest," I said.

"Quite acting like a big brother."

"No, I'm acting like the producer of the show. I order you to take five."

I fetched the bottle of brandy that I'd stuck in the back of a kitchen cabinet, a chilled bottle of O'Doul's, and two glasses. We sat on the sofa in the living room. I put the brandy glass in her hands. We started with some small talk. I told her about my recent visit with our parents and that Father's orchestra was floundering financially. She hadn't heard that bit of news. In turn, she informed me about all the wonderful things my fantastic brother was doing—as if I cared.

Then I said, "I want to ask you a question. You don't have to answer it."

"What is it?"

"What made you decide to do this gig?"

She hung her head for a moment and warmed the brandy in her hands. "For the money."

"That's it? Just that?"

"You don't know what it's like living on nothing. You've never had to scrape by. You have this nice house and everything you want. You've never had to choose which utility to cut for the month because you coulndn't pay them all. You don't have a landlord who raises your rent every year. You're not praying for the postman to arrive that day with your government check so you can eat."

"How do you get by?"

"Father pays me a stipend every month and that helps. Warren gives me money as well."

And you don't. She didn't say it, but I heard it loud and clear.

"If you need money, you can always ask."

"I'm tired of handouts and feeling like a beggar. I want to make it on my own." She drained the glass and held it out for me to take. "Back to work."

"Sure." I took her glass and we both stood up. "I'm going to bed now. I'll lock up, and you can quit whenever you're ready. 'Night, Sis."

"What was it I said to you when we were kids? 'Nighty night, numbskull.'"

I smiled. "Don't stay up too late, okay?"

Either Celeste didn't hear me, or she ignored me. She plugged the headphones into the instrument so the music wouldn't bother me, and her fingers once more flew over the keys.

The next morning, I found her draped over the keyboard, snoozing. I shook her shoulder. "Hey, wake up." She raised her head and rubbed her eyes. "What did you do, play lullabies?"

"Did I doze off?" She ran her fingers over the face of her Braille watch.

"It's six in the morning. Have you been here all night?"

"I guess so."

"I'm going to the gym now. I'll pick you up later for rehearsal. Now go to bed. I mean it. You won't do me any good if you fall asleep while I'm singing."

"No, I need to go over this one more—"

"I just pulled the plug on the keyboard. Now, off to bed

before I carry you up the stairs."

"Can I at least have some breakfast first? I'm not the one on the starvation diet."

MONDAY: Jacksonville, Florida
Chapter 4: Everybody Come Aboard

During the early morning hours of the day of the cruise, Celeste and I took a flight from LAX to the port in Jacksonville, Florida. On the plane, I watched a movie and chatted with the other guests in first class. Celeste slept most of the way, no doubt exhausted from our extensive rehearsals. She had on a nice slacks suit as well as the dark glasses she wore in public. I sported sandals along with brand new shirt and shorts—between my skimpy diet and daily workouts, I'd dropped several pounds into a smaller size. I looked better, felt better.

After we landed, we ate a quick lunch in an airport restaurant and took a shuttle to the port for boarding. One perk for the headline entertainers was that officials sped us through for embarkation, and we avoided the long wait with the regular passengers in line. Once on the ship, a porter showed us to our rooms—two adjoining suites with a connecting door and private balconies on the Capricorn Deck. In keeping with the ship's name, the public areas and decks were named for the zodiac signs.

A fruit and chocolate basket with champagne awaited in our respective cabins. I gave my bottle to Celeste and kept the fruit for a late night snack. Later that night, I donated the candy to the band members who had less lavish accommodations on the Horoscope Deck two levels below. Musicians were always starving, and feeding them made them happy.

While waiting for our luggage to arrive and before the

ship filled up with people, Celeste and I took a survey walk of the vessel. She wanted to memorize the layout of the ship and pace out the distance between the elevators and the various rooms. Celeste held my elbow as I led her along the best travel routes. She made notes to herself on a handheld tape recorder. Most of the rooms we'd be using were clustered on two decks, so she wouldn't need to travel far between floors.

Celeste was born blind due to a birth defect. In that year, 1960, medical research wasn't as advanced as today, and the doctors couldn't help her. But my parents were undeterred, and they worked hard to give her a good upbringing. My stay-at-home mother refused to put Celeste in a school for the blind and home schooled her instead, which could be why my sister never learned to be comfortable around large groups and strangers. She had piano lessons just like her brothers. The family was more protective of Celeste than necessary. We often spoiled her, but overall, she was just one of the clan. Warren and I played and fought with her like any batch of siblings.

As we explored our new home for the next week, I found our performing venue. My name and recently updated headshot graced the entrance to the Leo Lounge, on the Astrology Deck just below the open air Lido Deck topside. I didn't tell Celeste that the glass wall frame only held my photo, not hers, and her name was in miniscule letters at the bottom of the "Now Appearing" display. We went inside to scope out the space. When Marshall said the venue was "intimate," he wasn't kidding; I'd seen larger doghouses. About fifty people could squeeze around the tables in front of the postage-stamp-sized stage only a couple of feet above the floor. I wondered how we'd stuff all the musicians and instruments onto that tiny stage. I was also irked that the management didn't think I deserved the larger venue right next door, the Sagittarius Showroom.

"Sis, you're lucky that you're blind."

"Why's that?"

"You don't have to look at the tacky décor."

Yes, in keeping with the room's name, huge black-and-white, floor-to-ceiling photos of prowling tigers graced the walls. On entering the lounge, one had to step on a fake tiger skin rug. A tiger-stripe pattern was embedded into the plastic tabletops. The chairs and wall lights were bright orange with black trim. If the ocean waves didn't make me seasick, I'd get ill just looking at the furnishings every night. We headed backstage and, to my relief, the dressing rooms—one room for me, another for Celeste and a third for the band—were normal with white walls, lighted mirrors and no kitsch.

We ended our ship's tour in our rooms. The suites were roomy enough, with a double bed, table, a writing desk attached to the wall, chairs and a small sofa. Unlike the flashy Leo Lounge, our staterooms were blah, with tan walls, nondescript furniture and tacky wall paintings of ancient sailing ships. I tucked my wallet into my room's wall safe because I wouldn't need cash, credit cards or my driver's license for the next week—any expenses beyond our comps would get charged to my room for me to pay on the final day. Celeste, who never left the house without a purse, had brought a fanny pack to wear around her waist. She was afraid someone might snatch a purse off her shoulder.

I sat on a chair in my sister's suite while she unpacked her clothes and hung them in the closet in a specific order. Celeste had tiny Braille tags inside her clothes so she could match colors and styles.

"The ship's so big." I heard a note of fear in her voice.

"Of course. It's a city at sea with about a thousand people onboard. I hope you're not going to spend all your time hiding in here."

"It's just—"

"Wait. I have something for you." I ducked into my suite through the connecting door and returned with a small object that I placed in her hands.

"What's this?" she asked.

"It's a two-way radio. Carry this with you at all times. If you run into trouble, call me."

"I won't need this."

"I insist."

"If you say so."

The gray battery-powered walkie-talkie had a short, thick antenna. The captain, who was aware of Celeste's disability, had given me permission to use the devices onboard the ship. We probably wouldn't need them, but I figured Celeste would feel safer if she had a lifeline to me. She placed the communication device in her fanny pack. I had a leather holder on my belt for my receiver.

At three o'clock, we returned to the Leo Lounge for a quick run-through of the show. By now the instruments were in place, which left only a teensy patch of stage for yours truly to strut his stuff. Frank, the band and Jackson Meers, the road manager, were present. Jackson was in charge of a myriad of details including, but not limited to: setting up everything needed for the shows, handling the merchandise, keeping spare guitar strings on hand, operating the sound/light board since the budget didn't allow for a tech guy, and running errands for Celeste and me.

We set a level on the instruments. I walked through my dance numbers. Celeste, perched behind the Yamaha, seemed nervous.

"Sis, are you all right?"

"I can't believe I'm doing this. All those people will be staring at me."

"Look at it this way. If anyone falls asleep during the

show, you won't notice."

She laughed, and that broke the tension. I had opening night jitters as well. I hadn't performed a solo show in decades and never for an older audience that found Perry Como exciting. Would they enjoy a faded teen idol singing about puberty love? With the audience so close to the stage, I'd see every bored face and wristwatch glance. If we bombed tonight, Celeste and I might simply jump into a lifeboat and row to shore.

When we finished the rehearsal, Celeste and I returned to our rooms. The SS Zodiac set sail at four o'clock with a full complement of vacationers ready to hang loose and have fun. Shortly after the behemoth launched, the ceiling intercoms announced a mandatory lifeboat drill for all crew and passengers. I helped Celeste find the life jacket in her cabin. I grabbed mine as well, and we headed for the Lido Deck where a crewmember instructed us on what to do during an emergency—which, of course, he assured us, was highly unlikely to ever happen due to the superior construction of the ship and the cruise line's excellent safety record. We had to put on our life jackets and then wear them for the duration of the talk. A life jacket is the most constricting and uncomfortable clothing item ever devised except for certain female undergarments. If I were adrift, I'd rather sink than risk getting choked by this orange monstrosity.

When a wiseacre teenager asked if the movie "Titanic" would be screened during the trip, the crewmember gave him an icy stare and a curt "No!" He then lectured us about using the shipboard hospital if we had an aliment or sea sickness; warned us about communicable diseases and urged us to wash our hands often and practice good hygiene; and to be careful with our valuables and watch out for potential pickpockets. On that happy note, he dismissed us with a wish for a pleasant voyage.

To cheer up the passengers after that dismal pep talk, everyone was invited to a meet and mingle party in the Cosmic Atrium, two levels below on the Astrology Deck. Celeste and I dropped off our life jackets—which we hoped we'd never have to set eyes on again—in our cabins.

Celeste was not happy at leaving her room again so soon. "Do we have to go?"

"We need to get out and about to drum up interest in our show."

"I don't like getting jostled around in crowds."

"The atrium has chairs and tables. You can sit down and stay put. We won't be long, just enough to put in an appearance. Besides, if you do this, I have a surprise for you."

"What kind of surprise?"

"If I told you, it wouldn't be a surprise."

The Cosmic Atrium was simply a large open space, the social "hub" in the center of the ship with the various lounges and activity rooms radiating from it. In keeping with the ship's theme, the floor had midnight blue carpeting emblazoned with an enormous gold astrology wheel. The tables and chairs were white frosted Lucite embedded with gold stars. Hundreds of shiny gold streamers with silver stars dangled from the ceiling. In the room's apex, a crescent-shaped moon slowly rotated, occasionally shooting off "rays" of light.

I described this to Celeste. She laughed. "I could do a better job of decorating the ship."

"I'm sure you could."

Celeste sat at a table while I fetched drinks from the mile-long frosted plastic counter. I grabbed a glass of wine for Celeste (she only drank brandy at night) and a bottle of chilled water for myself. As I wove through the noisy crowd on my way to our table, I searched in vain for Cinnamon. With so many people milling around, I probably missed her. Or maybe she was unpacking or she had decided to skip the party. Or maybe she and her boyfriend were steaming up their cabin porthole—

A familiar voice cut through the hubbub. "Sandy! Sandy! There you are! Hi!"

"Who's that?" Celeste asked.

I was standing by the table. "I'll be dogged. It's Bunny McAllister, president of my fan club, and it looks like she brought an army with her."

Bright and beaming, my number one fan ran up with about a dozen young women following in her wake. Short and plump, in her thirties, with short frizzy brown hair and rimless glasses, Bunny might not win a beauty pageant, but she was a loyal fan. She managed to pop up wherever I was performing. She knew everything I was doing because she published the *Dreamy Detective* fanzine for the members of Sandy's Buddies fun club.

She gazed at me with undying devotion. "Wow, Sandy, this is so exciting! I've never been on a cruise before! Some girls from the fan club came along too. I reserved a block of rooms so we'd all be together. We can't wait to see your show tonight!"

"Hi, Bunny. Don't tell me you took another week off from your job for this."

"Uh huh. I have loads of vacation time stack up. I knew that someday you'd be performing again, and I wanted to be ready!"

Bunny introduced me to some of her friends. I noticed Celeste was getting fidgety. I suppose she had a right to be angry with me for hogging the glory while she was snubbed.

"Girls, I want you to meet my sister, Celeste Farmington. She'll be singing with me tonight."

"Oh, hi, Celeste! I've read all about you!" Bunny probably knew more about my family tree than I did. "It's great to meet a member of Sandy's family! Welcome aboard!"

"Hello." Celeste sounded a bit wary.

As the ladies greeted my sister, Bunny said to me, "So, Sandy, are you going to solve another mystery?"

"What mystery? Where?"

"Here on the ship. You know, like you did at my Beatles convention and when you were on that TV show."

"I certainly hope not. Celeste and I are here to do our show and to enjoy ourselves, nothing more. I hope you gals have a good time, too."

"Oh, we will! We will!"

The fans finally dispersed, and I sat at the table with Celeste. "So, how did you like your taste of stardom?"

She fanned herself with her drink napkin. With all the people milling about and since the air conditioning had only just kicked in, the room was stuffy. "Your fans are rather enthusiastic, aren't they?"

"They're good kids. I'm glad they're here. At least we won't be playing to an empty house."

Before I could touch my bottled water, I suffered another interruption. A flash of light went off, and that could only mean one thing—a photographer. Out of habit, I turned my face in the direction of the camera flash and smiled. It's not that I'm vain (not much), only that photo taking was a constant occurrence in my heyday; I learned to take it in stride.

"Hey, Sis, look this way."

"Why?"

"Someone's taking our picture."

"Oh, my."

She managed a half-hearted smile as the flash went off again. Cameras made Celeste sensitive since she couldn't tell if she took a good shot. The photographer, who had a large, expensive camera, handed me a card and announced that prints of the shots would be available for purchase as souvenirs in the photo gallery on the Constellation Deck below. The picture takers would be roaming the ship all week long, taking candid and posed shots of everyone onboard. I tucked the card into the pocket of my shorts. I had a feeling my fans would be snatching up all the pictures of their idol.

Other people gathered around the table; some of the passengers had recognized me. I made a point to introduce Celeste, but the guests didn't seem interested in her. As usual, a few folks confused me with Shaun Cassidy from TV's *The Hardy Boys Mysteries* (no, we blonds don't all look alike). Then a stunning bit of eye candy sided up to me, a gorgeous brunette in a tight low-cut dress. I couldn't wait to get to the pool and see this creature in a bikini. I gave her my full attention and a big smile.

She spoke in a loud voice. "That girl at the table is blind, isn't she? What's this cruise line coming to if they hire cripples for the entertainment?"

I frowned. "Yes, she's blind, but she isn't deaf. Or dumb. That's my sister. She's performing in my show."

My comment didn't faze Miss Rude Remarks. "I didn't need to rely on nepotism to get cast in the Starlight Ocean Revue on this ship. Just talent."

"How interesting. That's how I started my career too. With talent."

Miss Brain-dead gave me an angry look. I moved away and struck up a conversation with a nice-looking couple. I glanced at Celeste. Thankfully, she was too busy hobnobbing with an older woman to hear the crass remark. I glanced at my watch. I needed to get Celeste out of here and then change clothes before dinner—shorts were not allowed in the dining room. Besides, she was clearly overwhelmed by the socializing. I touched Celeste on the back of her hand, our signal for her to take my arm. She gripped my elbow and we walked away. I didn't mind escorting her—I loved having a beautiful woman on my arm.

We stepped into one of the glass-sided elevators that ran through the public decks. I hit the "up" button and the door closed. I told Celeste we were alone, so we could talk freely.

"Why are we going up?" she asked. "Our cabins are below."

"Your surprise is up on the Recreation Deck.

"What? There's nothing there but the gym, the spa and—"

"The beauty salon. I made an appointment for you to have the works. Facial, manicure, pedicure, shampoo—"

"But, Ernest! We have the show tonight."

"I know. That's why I want you to look your best. The salon promised they'd have you ready in time. Dinner will be waiting in your dressing room when you're finished."

"Ernest, thank you. That's wonderful."

"Besides, I didn't like the idea of you eating alone in your cabin."

"You could always stay with me."

"Sorry, but meeting the public is part of my job."

"You love all this attention, don't you?"

"As a matter of fact, I do."

That's the trouble with being a star. Once you get used to the spotlight it's impossible to live without it, and our glow fades when people stop looking at us.

"Don't forget," I added, "we need you backstage by seven-forty-five. Jackson will pick you up. You have your two-way radio?"

"Stop fussing, Ernest. If I need you, I'll telegraph an SOS and wave a signal flag."

I smiled. Celeste was starting to sound like her old feisty self. I left her at the salon and made a quick stop at my cabin to change into shoes, a collarless white shirt, a leisure suit and pants before heading to the Aries Dining Room on the Astrology Deck where I was about to hit some turbulence.

Chapter 5: Do You Know Who I Am?

The ship was chugging along and would continue through the night until it reached Key West on Tuesday. Now that we were farther out at sea, the water turned choppy. The deck below my feet rocked slightly, just enough to remind me I was no longer on solid ground. I felt dizzy from the motion of the waves—was I getting seasick? The sensation passed but I wondered how Celeste was holding up. What if she was too queasy to perform tonight? What if our audience turned green as well? Maybe we should stock the Leo Lounge with barf bags.

The atrium was in the ship's bow (front). From the atrium, a corridor ran down the center of the ship to the Aries Dining Room in the stern (rear). The various entertainment venues lined both sides of this hallway, which made it handy for passengers to bop in and sample all the shows—and leave early if they didn't like what they saw. In the dining room, the guests were assigned the same tables and sitting times for the duration of the cruise. One could be scheduled for either the main sitting at six o'clock or the late sitting at eight-fifteen.

The entertainers had the early sitting, of course, since our first show of the night started at eight-forty-five followed by a repeat performance at ten-thirty to accommodate the late diners. The headliners like myself ate in a small room off the main dining hall for privacy. I found out later that the DJs employed for the Scorpio Disco chowed down along with the common folk. Apparently, even cruise lines had a ranking system for the talent.

Inside the dining room, I spotted my band seated at a table and I stopped by to say hello. I wasn't going to eat with them, but not out of spite. During my touring days, I never got close to the bands in my shows. I always traveled separately for security reasons, and I usually never saw the guys until I actually stepped on stage. The maître d' led me to the private room off to one side. I was curious to meet the other acts on the ship, although I couldn't imagine why the passengers would want to see anyone else except me.

This smaller room was somewhat free of the Aries theme save for the fake sheepskin covering the backs of the chairs and the oh-so-cute ram-and-ewe ceramic salt-and-pepper shakers on the table. The twelve zodiac signs decorated the rims of the china plates and saucers, but the metal cutlery and the white tablecloth were normal enough. The maitre d' left me to my own devices. So far, the room only had two occupants beside myself.

"So where the tarnation is that little she-devil?"

The stocky man drawled in an accent as thick as a bowl of cooked grits. He was a couple of inches taller than myself—I stand at six-foot-two, so he was an imposing figure—solid muscle without a bit of fat. He wore a western-style shirt, a black bolo tie held in place with a silver buffalo skull clip, a fringed brown buckskin jacket and, yes, cowboy boots. A Stetson hat was on the table next to one of the place settings. I wasn't aware the ship had a Wild West Show—if so, I'd bet on this guy to win at bull wrestling.

The other occupant spoke. "Chill, man. She'll be along directly. We don't have to wait for Miss Prissy Pants to arrive before we start eating." This guy was tall but lean to the point of anorexia; his face pale from spending too many days inside venues. His slicked back, jet-black hair was an obvious dye job. Long, slender fingers adjusted the flower in the lapel of his suit.

The cowboy spotted me. "Well, lookie here! A new guest! Howdy, partner!" If he ever milked a cow the way he squeezed my hand, that Bessie would kick him to the moon.

"Careful with the hand, Tex. I'm playing guitar tonight." I squirmed under his crushing grip.

"Sorry, don't know my own strength sometimes." To my relief, he released my hand. To my chagrin, he slapped me on the back hard enough to dislodge anything stuck in my throat. "Just wanted to give you a right friendly welcome. Looks like you're the virgin on this here boat."

"Excuse me?" I wasn't sure if I should be amused or insulted.

"He means this is your first cruise aboard the floating fantasy world known as the Zodiac," the other man interjected. "It is, isn't it?"

"Yes, you're right." I shook the second man's hand. He must use some fantastic type of hand cream because his skin was soft as satin sheets. "And you are—?"

"Tommy Driswell, piano man extraordinary of the Pisces Piano Bar. The guests can't name a tune that I can't play."

"What about *Girl of My Dreams*?" My hit single of 1975 that launched my career into the stratosphere.

He laughed. "You naughty boy; you don't fool me a bit. You're Sandy Fairfax, aren't you?"

"Guilty as charged. I'll be in the Leo Lounge."

"Ah, the Leo Lounge. Aptly named. That dismal room has devoured many a performer." Not what I wanted to hear in my attempt to restart my lagging career. "So, Sandy, why don't you drop by the Pisces after your show and we can share a few duets?"

What a ghastly idea. "I won't be finished until after eleven-thirty."

"No problem at all. I'll be tickling the ivories until one

a.m."

By that time, the only thing I want to be tickling would be the pillow on my bed.

The Texan finally introduced himself. "All right, you boys have been ignoring me for long enough. Rex Stevenford is the name, and magic is my game." He reached behind my ear and produced a silver coin. An old cliché but effective. "Huh? How's that?"

"Do that a few more times and I'll be able to pay my band."

He let out a hardy guffaw. "That's rich! You're all right, Sandy Fairfax."

"So you have a magic show onboard?" I was hoping he'd do a trick now, such as disappear from the room.

"Yes, siree, bob, the best act of the Starlight Ocean Revue in the Sagittarius Showroom."

This rodeo clown nabbed the largest venue onboard while I was stuck in a broom closet? Before I could reply, a woman strolled into the room—the rude person I'd met in the atrium earlier.

"Speak of the devil!" Rex said. "There she is! Jodie, allow me to introduce—"

She glared at me. "We've met."

I was dumbfound by the irony of once more meeting someone I never wanted to see again. I gave her a nod. "Ma'am."

"I'll be hornswoggled," said Rex. "Must be a mighty small boat if the two of you bumped into each other on the very first day."

Tommy added his observations. "Sandy, this is Miss Jodie Russ, the diva of the revue, and she'll never let you forget it."

"Oh lay off, Tommy," she snapped. At least I wasn't the only person onboard she disliked. "I'm not feeling well, and I'm not in the mood for your cat claws."

"Meow, meow," he replied. "You're the expert at the feline frolics, my dear, not I."

She eyed the pianist and said in a low voice, "We need to talk later."

He forced a smile, but he sounded worried. "But of course."

Rex grinned. "Let's not squabble in front of our guest. We don't want him to think we're all a bunch of rattlesnakes, now do we? What's the matter, Jodie, feeling seasick? Or is Montezuma taking his revenge already?"

"I'm just tired."

"We've barely raised the anchor, missy. How can you be tuckered out already?"

"I'm sick and tired of Hugh. He says I'm getting too old for the show. He wants to replace me. With whom? His brainless bedroom bimbo? I tell him it's not age—it's experience. Show me a nineteen-year-old who can deliver the show as well as I can."

"No argument there, missy," said Rex. "I've never heard a nightingale warble as well as you. You're the finest tunesmith onboard this ship, bar none." He glanced at me. "The finest female singer, that is."

She sat at the table and the men grabbed the remaining chairs. I made sure I was on the opposite side of the table from her. Going clockwise around the table we had: Jodie, two empty chairs, yours truly, Tommy, two more unoccupied chairs, and Rex beside the diva.

I said to the pianist, "I'm left-handed. Do you want to change chairs so I don't bump you while I'm eating?"

"No, you're fine. I can adapt. I'm an expert at working with whatever life throws at me."

The waiter came in to hand out the menus, fill our water glasses, and take our orders. The rich dishes on the bill of fare sounded tempting, but if I started gaining weight, I wouldn't fit into my already tight black leather concert pants. Besides, I could never eat a heavy meal right before a show. I settled for coffee and a grilled organic chicken breast salad. However, after the shows I planned on attacking the midnight pasta buffet with gusto. The waiter left after taking the orders, and the conversations resumed. Rex and Jodie talked shop about changes in the revue, so I turned my attention to Tommy.

"I take it all of you have worked this cruise before?"

"Many times, anywhere the Zodiac sails. I'll probably grow old and meet my Maker aboard this ship. They can just tie my broken old bones to the anchor and bury me at sea."

"Have you thought about working a job on land?"

"You know Billy Joel's song *Piano Man*? Been there, done that. At least on a cruise you get a fresh batch of faces every week or two, not the same old sorry broken-down crowd. And most of them tip well. Folks loosen up the purse strings when they're on vacation. So what's your story? How does a champion show dog like yourself end up among us flea-bitten mutts?"

"That's a long story, Tommy."

"All right by me. You've got five days to tell it."

A newcomer entered the room—a sweet, lovely young lady, early twenties I'd say, large brown eyes and hair to match. She wore an attractive dress. All of the men stood up. Jodie stayed seated and sipped from her water glass.

Rex said to the girl, "May I present Sandy Fairfax, joining us for his very first Zodiac cruise. My stage assistant and the apple of my eye, my daughter, Nessie."

I leaned over the table to shake her hand "Hello, Nessie, my pleasure." How did this coarse man produce such a delicate flower?

"Hi, Sandy," she replied. "I heard you were joining us. I'm a quite a fan."

"Thank you. I wish you could see my show."

"Sorry, partner," Rex interrupted. "Nessie and I will be astounding the crowd in the showroom at the same time you'll be crooning in the lounge."

I bristled. "Wayne Newton croons. I *sing*."

Rex guffawed, but before he could make another stupid remark, the waiter arrived with our meals and we all sat. He placed a plate of beef stew in front of the empty chair to my right.

"Is someone else coming?" I asked.

The waiter nodded. I guess these performers had been around long enough that the staff knew their preferences. The daughter took the empty chair beside her father. The Texan had already ordered for Nessie, so we all started eating. I'm glad we didn't have to wait for her, because I was starved. I hadn't eaten since landing in Jacksonville in what seemed like years ago. I munched on my plate of greens—after weeks of salads I was ready to grow rabbit ears—while Tommy chatted about his bad old days of playing bar mitzvahs and corporate parties.

Then another colorful character joined us.

A middle-aged, rather mousey-looking guy dressed in an equally ordinary brown suit and tie hurried into the room. He carried a large, well-worn black suitcase. "Sorry I'm late, but Moze was being difficult just now."

Tommy made clicking noises of condolence. "Did you two have another spat?"

"He didn't think my new jokes were funny."

"What does he know?" Jodie said with a sneer. "He's such a blockhead!"

Silence fell on the room. The others stared at the diva for a moment and then went back to their meals. Rex and Nessie talked among themselves and ignored Jodie. The new guy sat in the open chair beside me and spoke to Tommy.

"Moze is very perceptive about these things. His comic

timing is impeccable. If he says a joke's off, it's off."

"Don't take it so hard," Tommy replied. "I'm sure you'll think of some better gags. Oh, where are my manners. This is Sandy Fairfax, the latest and greatest performer aboard our floating paradise."

New guy introduced himself as Aaron Goldstein, the comic scheduled for the Taurus Nightclub.

"I take it Moze is the partner in your act?" I asked.

"Yes, for fifteen years. Sometimes he's a handful to deal with, but he's the best in the business."

"Will he be joining us for dinner?"

The guy gave me a peculiar stare. "He's already here."

Aaron placed the suitcase on the chair to his right and opened it. He pulled out a ventriloquist's dummy and placed it on his left knee. The wooden creature had a dummy's exaggerated features, huge eyes and a smug expression. Aaron ate with his right hand while his left operated the dummy, which turned its face toward me.

"Hey, Fairfax." The dummy spoke in a high-pitched nasal voice. "You gonna get the little girls all hot and bothered at your gig tonight?"

Even though I knew who was really talking, I spoke directly to the dummy. "I beg your pardon?"

The dummy turned its head slightly toward Aaron, blinked, and then faced me again. "Aaron's jealous of you. He's not man enough to excite the ladies."

The comic looked at me with a sad expression. "I'm sorry, Sandy. Just try to ignore Moze."

"Why should he?" the dummy said. "I'm the most exciting dinner partner at this table. Welcome aboard, Sandy. You add some class to this otherwise sorry old crate."

I couldn't keep my eyes off the talking doll. I'd been around ventriloquists before—I had the pleasure of working with Jay Johnson when he guest-starred on my TV show a year before he hit it big with the smash comedy *Soap* in 1977—but I'd never met one who continued to playact off stage. Tommy leaned over to me and said something I didn't hear. He was speaking into my bad ear, the one that suffered hearing loss from my years of loud concerts.

I turned to face him. "What did you say?"

He nodded toward Aaron. "I said, just go with it."

Moze continued unabated between Aaron's bites of food. "This guy and I do a comedy act. He calls it a comedy act. I call it lame. Someday I'm gonna split this scene and hook up with some real talent."

Aaron gave an awkward laugh. "Now, Moze, you don't really mean it. We make a great team."

"So you say. If we're so hot, why are you still stuck on this rusty tugboat?"

"Please, Moze, don't upset me before show time."

"Hurry up and stuff your face, will ya? You need to change my clothes. I hate this outfit. Where did you get it, the Salvation Army store?"

"Yes, all right."

I wondered who was really pulling the strings in this bizarre relationship.

I finished eating, not only to escape this room of kooks, but so I could squeeze in a short powernap. During my hectic '70s heyday of nonstop recording, filming and concerts, I was an expert at zoning out any place, any time, for a short time and waking up refreshed and ready to go. I put my napkin on the table and excused myself.

"Before you hightail it out of here, Sandy," said Rex, "you might need this." He held up the keycard to my stateroom.

I said, "Where did you get—you picked my pocket, did you?"

He laughed. I took the keycard and shook my finger at

him in mock reproach. Good thing I didn't have my wallet on me. I left the dining room. In the hallway on the Capricorn Deck, en route to my stateroom, I passed several crewmembers pushing carts covered with white cloths and holding covered food trays. Apparently several well-heeled guests were dining privately in their suites. I reached my room, changed into casual clothes, and napped.

At seven-thirty-five, I awoke and called the salon. They were taking a little longer than anticipated for Celeste, but they would send her on her way as soon as possible. I rode the elevator two floors up to the Astrology Deck and walked through a door marked "Crew Only" that led to a special passageway. This narrow hallway ran along the perimeter of the deck to allow the performers and the crew private access to the venues.

In the Leo Lounge, I checked in with Frank and made sure my props were in place. In my dressing room, I found a clothes rack holding two sets of my stage clothes. I was pleased to see that the crew had provided my requested food and drink tray—chilled sodas, fruit drinks, PowerPunch energy drinks and O'Doul's; cheese and crackers; dried fruit and nuts; and chocolate candies—for my own snacking and for entertaining guests. Such snack trays were part of my contract with the cruise line and standard for celebrities working on the road—stardom has its perks.

A small vase of colorful flowers graced my makeup table as well. I read the attached card: "Have a terrific show tonight. You're awesome. Cinnamon."

My heart jumped. She liked me! I knew it! Obviously this stupid boyfriend meant nothing to her. I munched on a handful of nuts, opened a bottle of PowerPunch and changed into my stage clothes: a long-sleeved, cream-colored glitter shirt along with those gosh-awfully-snug black leather pants and my soft-soled black shoes. The last thing I needed on that wooden stage was the sound of me stomping around in hard soles. The hum of the ship's engines and the whoosh of the air through the cooling vents made a comforting white noise.

Jackson stopped by and helped me put on the hands-free microphone that looped over one ear. A cord ran from the earpiece down inside my shirt to the battery pack that rested on the small of my back. For most of the show, I'd be using a handheld mic to keep my hands from flailing around, but I needed the earpiece for my dance numbers. I marveled at this technology that wasn't available during my teen idol years.

After Jackson left, I combed my hair and retied my ponytail. Then a pit stop in the bathroom, along with brushing those pearly whites and a shot of breath spray. I sat in the black leather swivel chair in front of the wall mirror and applied my stage makeup. I have a faint scar on my left cheek, a sad memento of the night some years ago when a lush sliced my face with a broken beer bottle during a barroom brawl that I had started. I rubbed in some concealer to cover the mark.

I glanced at the wall clock—eight o'clock. No word from Celeste. I reached for the phone to call the salon again. Just then someone knocked on my door. I spun round in the swivel chair to face the doorway.

A familiar female voice said, "Can I come in? Are you decent?"

"Never around a pretty girl."

Cinnamon came into the room anyway. She had on a lovely knee-length evening dress that showed off a pair of delicious hose-clad calves. Nail-painted toes peeked out from the open-toe dress sandals. Dancers are blessed with beautiful legs.

"Thanks for the flowers. That was thoughtful of you." In my next sentence, I planned to ask her out for drinks after the second show.

"You're welcome. I hope Celeste likes hers too."

My heart sank. "You gave flowers to Celeste?"

"Sure. You're both performing tonight."

So much for my expectations. Cinnamon didn't mean anything special with the flowers—they were just a traditional showbiz opening night gesture.

"Are you nervous?" she asked.

"I'd be lying if I said no."

"You'll be great. I know it. Your dancing will knock their socks off."

The vessel began rocking slightly. "If this ship keeps rolling, my own socks might fall off as well." I turned the chair and gave myself a last minute check in the mirror. Was it my imagination or did I look tired? "What if nobody shows up? There's three other shows going on, plus all the games and whatnot for people to do. I'm nothing but a footnote on the list of daily activities."

Cinnamon stepped up behind me and put her hands on my shoulders, her green eyes on my mirror reflection. "Don't be so hard on yourself, Sandy. You've got a great show. Once the guests see you, they'll spread the word."

I kept staring into the mirror. "I'm worried about Celeste. What if she freezes or forgets the lyrics or—"

"Stop it, Sandy. Think positive thoughts and it'll all work out. Rah, rah, rah, go Sandy!"

I looked up at her. "Were you a cheerleader in high school?

"Matter of fact, I was."

"Then you can come and cheer for my team anytime." That line came out in a far more suggestive manner than I anticipated.

She laughed. "I need to go and help Celeste with her makeup. She should be here by now. Break a leg, Sandy." She gave my shoulders a squeeze before she left.

I stood and ran through my vocal warm-ups while I put on the last piece of my costume that brought Sandy Fairfax the entertainer to life. Around my neck went a blue satin scarf tied with a square knot. Back in the day, in a nod to my Buddy Brave character, I'd always worn a stupid scarf in concerts and most public appearances. I was going to forgo it this time, but Marshall, Frank, Cinnamon and Celeste had all demanded that I wear it (Celeste knew that Buddy wore a scarf because I used to complain about it so much).

Another knock on my door. I said come in, and Jackson did so. Since his work remained off stage, he was casually dressed in jeans and a Hawaiian shirt.

"Do you need anything, Sandy?"

"I'm fine, thanks. How's the house?"

"Your fan club camped outside in the hallway for an hour before we opened the doors so they'd be the first ones in." I expected that. "But it's early. We'll get more drifting in closer to curtain time. People are still finishing their dinners."

"If we have more people on stage than in the audience, I'm in a lot of trouble. Where's Celeste? Did you bring her back from the salon?"

"Yeah, but she looks a little ashen."

That didn't sound good. I thanked him and followed him out of my dressing room. I didn't lock the door, because I'd be zipping backstage halfway into the show for a quick costume change.

Celeste's room was next to mine. I knocked on the closed door. "Sis, it's Ernest. Can I come in?"

"Yes, please do." Only it was Cinnamon who answered, not my sister.

Puzzled, I opened the door. Cinnamon was standing beside the makeup table. My sister's dinner tray was still covered, apparently untouched.

"Where's Celeste?"

Cinnamon nodded at the closed bathroom door. From inside the privy came the sound of someone throwing up.

"Celeste says she can't do the show."

Chapter 6: A Whole Lot Of Shakin' Goin' On

"How long has she been in the can?" I asked.

"Since she arrived."

"That's just great." I tapped on the bathroom door and spoke as gently as I could, while keeping the anger out of my voice. My nerves were wound up enough already without this complication. Minutes before curtain wasn't the time to deal with a difficult performer.

"Sis? It's Ernest. Are you all right?"

A toilet flushed, and the door opened. Celeste was still in her street clothes. Jackson was right in that she looked pale—and terrified.

I took her hand. "I'm right here. Let's sit you down." I helped her to the swivel chair (her dressing room was identical to mine). "Are you seasick, or is it opening night jitters?"

"Both." She spoke in a hoarse whisper.

"I've got some Dramamine with me." Cinnamon rummaged in her purse. Off my look she said, "I've taken cruises before. I never travel without these." She took out a plastic pill bottle, popped the top, removed two tablets and folded my sister's fingers around them. "Chew these tablets. They'll stop that queasy feeling." Celeste put the pills in her mouth. "It might take a while to work, but you'll feel much better."

"Thanks." My sister began crying.

Cinnamon shot me a look. "Don't cry, Celeste, you'll do fine. We'll get you fixed up in your pretty clothes, and you'll look just great—"

"I want to go back to my room."

"Let me handle this." I moved Cinnamon out of the way, pulled up a stool, and sat beside Celeste. I held her hand as she sobbed. "Okay, first off, Sis, take a deep breath. Come on, breathe nice and easy. Good. Now listen to me. We've both worked very hard on this. We've come too far to quit. A lot of people are depending on us. There's an audience out there, and they're expecting you. The band needs you. I need you."

"I can't do it."

"Of course, you can. Look, forget about the audience. Just pretend it's only you and me playing together like when we were kids. Remember? We're alone in the living room at home, singing around the piano. Just the two of us, nobody else. Not even our stupid brother Warren." That got a little chuckle out of her. "Can you do that for me? Please?"

"I'll try."

"Good girl."

A knock from the hallway; I looked up, startled. I'd left the door open. Jackson stood in the doorway. "Sandy, Celeste, twenty minutes."

"Thank you," I said.

He glanced at Celeste and then at me. "Is she—?"

"We're fine. Thanks, Jackson." I motioned for him to leave. After he departed, I said to Celeste, "Come on, get your clothes on. You've got to hurry."

She wiped her mouth with the back of her hand. "I must look awful."

"That's okay. Lots of actors lose their lunch right before a show. Now pop in the bathroom and brush your teeth." After Celeste closed the bathroom door behind her, I said to Cinnamon, "Make sure she doesn't run off. Nail her feet to the floor if you have to. Can you get her ready in twenty minutes, or do we hold the curtain?"

"I've been in plays. I know how to make fast costume changes. Now shoo." She waved her hands at me in a brush-off gesture. "Men are not allowed in here while we're dressing."

I stepped into the hallway and closed the door behind me. The ship's entertainment director showed up to wish me well, although I think her motive was to make sure I was in the lounge earning my pay and not slumming in the casino. With nobody to talk to and nervous energy building up, I wandered around backstage. I greeted the band members as they came out from their dressing rooms. They were dressed alike in black cotton pants and red long-sleeved shirts—I made sure their shirts were a different color from my own. From beyond the backstage curtain, I heard the mumblings of the audience. At least someone was out there, alive and breathing.

Jackson said, "Five minutes, Sandy. Where's Celeste?"

"She's getting dressed."

"The staff is strict about the shows starting and stopping on time."

"She'll be here."

Jackson didn't look convinced, but he rounded up the band while I rapped on the dressing room door. Cinnamon opened the door.

"How is she?" I asked.

"See for yourself." She stepped aside as I entered the room. "Celeste, your brother's here."

Celeste stood up from the swivel chair. "How do I look?"

I gasped. "Like an angel."

She was quite the vision. In my previous panic I hadn't noticed what a nice job the salon had done with her. The beauticians had trimmed her nails and painted them bright red. Her hair was styled, hanging loose in soft waves around her face and shoulders. The color in her face had returned, and the makeup that Celeste had applied was stunning. The eye shadow and false lashes really brightened her face. Before we left L.A., Celeste and I had a heated argument about her not wearing her dark glasses on stage—I finally prevailed.

She wore a long black skirt and a gold blouse with long puffy sleeves and glittery threads that caught the light. A sprig of flowers was clipped in her hair. She didn't need a headset mic because she'd be sitting for the whole show; a mic stand had been set up beside her keyboard. As usual, Celeste had overloaded the jewelry—dangly gold earrings and sparkly gold neck chains and bracelets—but at this point I wasn't going to complain (she liked the jingly sound of all that hardware). We Farmingtons clean up nicely.

"Sis, I think you're going to upstage me."

Cinnamon said, "Celeste, I'll be back between shows to freshen your makeup. Now if you two will excuse me, I have to get my seat out front."

"You'll be watching the show?" I asked.

"Of course. I want to see how the dances turn out."

Celeste said, "I hope you and your boyfriend enjoy it."

"Garvin won't be with me. After dinner, he said he was tired and was going to lie down for a while. He was up late packing, and we had an early flight. He'll be joining me for drinks after the show."

I had to admit that was a relief. Not that her boyfriend was sick, but because I wouldn't have to watch the two of them playing footsie during my show.

Frank stepped up. "Celeste, it's Frank. It's time to go out front."

I added a last minute instruction. "Sis, one more thing. Don't forget, on stage you have to call me Sandy, not Ernest."

"It still doesn't sound right."

"Just make believe we're in a play and I'm playing a

dopey character named Sandy."

"The *dopey* part I can remember."

I grabbed her shoulders and lightly kissed her forehead, careful not to smudge her makeup. "Break a leg."

Jackson tapped my sister's arm and said in a loud whisper, "Go! Go! You're on!"

Frank placed my sister's hand on his elbow so he could lead her on stage. They walked around the backstage curtain; the other band members followed. Jackson went out front to run the soundboard and make the announcements over the lounge's intercom. At my request, Jackson told the audience that photography was allowed only during the first two songs. With the spectators sitting on top of the stage, I didn't need camera flashes going off in my eyes all night. Left alone, I was nearly flattened with a bout of stage fright. Fussing over Celeste had momentarily taken my mind off my own anxiety. How was *I* going to get through the night?

The band played a lively intro, a medley of my hits to get the audience wound up. Jackson announced over the intercom, "And now, ladies and gentlemen, the Leo Lounge and Zodiac Cruise Line is proud to present for your entertainment tonight the star of screen and stage, with ten gold records and eight number one pop hits—teen idol, musician, actor and the world's greatest boy sleuth. Please welcome—Sandy Fairfax!"

The band struck up a rousing version of my TV show's theme song. I ran onstage, grabbed the hand microphone off the stand and smiled at my audience. Gosh, it felt incredible to be back in front of a crowd. My fan club filled the tables closest to the stage. They greeted me with ear-piercing screams and a barrage of camera flashes. Apparently they missed the memo that said they were no longer in a super-size stadium, and I could hear them just fine at a lower volume.

Even with the stage lights on, I could see most of the tables in the room. The population in the back of the lounge was sparse with a few couples scattered here and there, with far too much room left over for latecomers. The back section greeted me with polite, gentle applause. I'd have to work hard to cheer them up. I spotted Cinnamon sitting near the front and grinned at her. She smiled back and gave me a little wave. The wait staff continued to take and fill drink orders among the tables—quite distracting, but then again, with a few scotch-and-sodas under their belts the lackluster crowd might loosen up and enjoy the show.

I launched into a trio of my upbeat hits. The band sounded great. As I sang, I glanced over my shoulder at Celeste. She was perched on a bench behind the Yamaha keyboard, so focused on her music I doubted that she even heard the audience. Between the numbers, I threw in jokes and stories about my Good Old Days. The cowlick kept falling in my face—that happened whenever I moved too fast—but I ignored it. I slowed the pace with some ballads. I picked up an acoustic guitar for a solo version of a Beatles number, *In My Life,* a nod to the influence of the Fab Four on my life and also homage to a song that meant much to me.

Time for the duet part of the show. Right on cue and according to the script, Celeste said, "Excuse me, Sandy, haven't you been hogging the stage long enough?"

I pretended I was hurt. "What do you mean? Isn't this the Sandy Fairfax show?"

"Well, *I'm* here."

"So you are. You always liked to tag along with your big brother. Ladies and gentlemen, may I present the finest girl singer I know, as well as the prettiest. She's also my kid sister, but don't hold that against her. Please welcome—Celeste Farmington!"

I was grateful for my fan club, because they responded

warmly. The rest of the audience, no doubt groggy from the heavy dinners, barely touched their palms together. Thank goodness Celeste didn't see the lack of enthusiasm in the house, or she would have folded. She nodded in the direction of the tables and continued with the script.

"Why don't you let me sing for a while and give the audience a chance to wake up?"

"They're not asleep." I looked at the band. "Are they?" The musicians closed their eyes and made loud snoring noises.

Celeste said, "I think the band's getting ready for the all-night poker tourney in the casino."

"I hope they win big. Then I won't have to pay them. All kidding aside, folks, I'm going to join Celeste for a duet."

She scooted over on the bench, and I sat beside her. A hot spotlight fell on us. Celeste blinked under the glare— she can sense bright light. In L.A., we hadn't rehearsed with a spotlight. I hoped it wouldn't throw her off.

Then she said, "You've put on some weight, Sandy. You never used to take up so much space on the bench."

That, my friends, was an unexpected ad-lib. During rehearsals she never strayed from the script. I was so surprised I stared at her, my mouth gaping. My fan club giggled. Not only was Celeste one-upping me, but getting the laughs. She grinned and pounced into the song intro before I could think up a snappy comeback. I had no choice but to start singing. If Celeste was nervous, she didn't show it. She sang with confidence and not a single glitch. When we finished, the audience was generous in its applause. Her face beamed—I hadn't seen her this happy in a long time. I gave her hand a little squeeze to let her know I was pleased.

"Well, Celeste, that was pretty good. Now that you're warmed up, how about doing something all by yourself?"

Even though that line was scripted, she acted as if I was

asking her for real. "Sure, Sandy, I'd love to. And I have just the song ready."

I moved to the side of the stage while she played and sang one of her songs from days gone by, a tender love piece she'd written in the '70s. I'd forgotten just how sweet her voice sounded. The song was more than her time to shine—I needed to get ready for my big dance number. I always scheduled it early in the show while I was still fresh and not too worn out. Out of the range of the spotlight, I set the hand mic back in the stand and switched into my tap shoes for the *Top Hat And Tails* number. The person who had invented Velcro straps on shoes in place of laces should be canonized. I picked up my props—a black satin top hat and a thin cane wrapped in silver tape. Normally, I did this number in a soft-shoe shuffle, but with the metal taps my sister could hear me move and keep up with the music. At the soundboard, Jackson switched on my head mic so I could sing.

The dance number went well until the ship hit a wave and the floor shifted beneath my feet. I lost my footing, stumbled and fumbled the lyrics as well. Of course, the die-hard fans noticed—they'd memorized every word and note of my songs—and gasped. The band kept going. I improvised some steps until I caught up with the musicians.

After that bit, we'd reached the midpoint of the show. Celeste had another solo spot, which gave me a good excuse to rush backstage and change clothes. I'd worked up a sweat in *Top Hat And Tails* and needed dry clothes. Plus, a change of costume gave the audience some new eye candy, and I needed to rest my voice. In my dressing room, I closed the door, stripped off my shirt and scarf and left them on the floor—Jackson would pick them up later to deliver to the ship's cleaning service. I donned a blue glitter shirt and a white silk scarf as well as changed back into my soft-soled shoes. I also downed a hefty swig of chilled water and mopped the sweat off my face. The song ran exactly three minutes, thirty-five seconds, so I moved like a whirlwind. Not much time to catch my breath. My sister's song came through the room's intercom that fed the show backstage. I kept track of the time by listening to the singing.

As she hit the final note of the song, I returned to the stage and encouraged the audience to give Celeste a hand. The last half of the show flew by as the audience began to perk up. I asked *Buddy Brave* trivia questions. I did a survey of where people were from and what they were doing when they first heard one of my songs on the radio, and embarrassed the life out of a honeymooning couple (nothing too naughty, mind you).

"Well, folks, hate to sing and run, but our time's up and the cleaning crew is at the door. Thanks for sharing your time with us. We hope to leave you with some joy in your heart and a smile on your face. If you're off to hit the bars, please be responsible and don't drink and walk on the way home. That's all the songs I know, so there isn't anything more for me to do."

I hoped the die-hard fans would realize I hadn't yet performed one of my biggest hits. Sure enough, as if prompted, Bunny shouted, "*Girl of My Dreams!*"

I leaned over the edge of the stage to speak to her. "What?"

"*Girl of My Dreams!* You didn't do *Girl of My Dreams!*"

"*Girl of My Dreams?*" I turned to the band. "Have you guys ever heard of a song called *Girl of My Dreams?*" They shook their heads.

"Sandy, I think I know that one," Celeste said.

"Really? How does it go?"

She tootled a few bars on the keyboard and the fans cheered.

"It sounds nice. Keep playing, Sis. I'll pick it up as you go along."

The band struck up the accompaniment, I sang, and we finished the show. I bowed and my fan club gave me a standing ovation. Some of the girls handed me gifts— flowers, stuffed animals, cards of appreciation and scrapbooks. I put the items to the side of the stage to take back to my stateroom later. I took Celeste's hand and led her out front for her bow. We did a bow together and I wrapped up with one more on my own. The applause started dying down, so I left the stage quickly with Celeste in tow.

Backstage, I gave her a big hug. "Sis, you were fantastic!"

"Did we really do it? It seems so surreal."

"Aren't you glad I talked you into this?"

"I feel so jazzed. Wow. It's exciting. They really liked us, didn't they?"

"What's not to like? A pretty gal, a handsome guy–"

"Who's the handsome guy?"

"By the way, about that ad-lib of yours during the duet—I'm warning you, I'll be thinking up some quips of my own before the next show."

Her face fell. "We have to do this all over again, don't we?"

"Yes, but don't worry about that now. Let's go out front and meet the fans."

I took Celeste back into the lounge. Most of the audience had beaten a hasty retreat to the bars and the casino, but my fan club and a few other interested persons were still hanging around, enjoying the afterglow. Jackson had set up a folding table for autograph signings and selling merchandise. We couldn't bring too many items aboard, so we settled on eight-by-ten glossy pix of me, both current and Buddy Brave circa 1977, and two of my albums on

CD, *Sandy Sings Live for You* and *Sandy's Tastiest Treats* (greatest hits).

We'd managed to dig up my sister's two albums on cassette tapes, *A Dragon in the Forest* and *Gently Sings the Dove*—nobody had transferred them to CD yet. Jackson handled the sales and money while Celeste and I sat and chatted with the fans. Some of them had brought their own album covers and knickknacks for me to sign. I'm sure some of the fans bought my sister's tapes only because of her connection with me, but I didn't care as long as her merchandise moved. I posed for a few fan photos until the cleaning crew really did move in to prepare the lounge for the second show.

By now, Celeste had her appetite back. Jackson dashed off to the Gemini Bar and Grill to get her a fresh sandwich (the dinner previously left in her dressing had gone cold). I returned to my dressing room to relax, nibble on the snacks and schmooze with some of the ship's VIPs. After they left, I took a quick shower (yes, I took off the headset first) and changed into clean clothes for the second show. After I was dressed and set up with the mic, Cinnamon entered the room and hugged me.

"Sandy, how wonderful! What an incredible show! You were fantastic! And your sister is such a trouper and so amazing. Why isn't she out performing and recording?"

I ignored the question. "How did you like *Top Hat and Tails*?"

"Pretty good, except for that new step you put in the middle."

"It's not my fault the ship when one way while my feet went another. Next time, I'm going to practice these dances while standing on a teeter-totter."

"Look, I have some ideas for improving the dances. Can we meet tomorrow for a quick run-through?"

"Yeah, sure."

"All right. We'll catch up tomorrow. Now I have to find Garvin. He should be up by now."

She left. I couldn't figure what she saw in a guy who came on a cruise and then hid in his room during the busiest part of the day.

Just before the second show started, I reminded Celeste not to get complacent and to keep her energy up. Sometimes performers get too relaxed after a good opening and phone in the next show. This time, we had a slightly larger audience, no doubt picking up people from the late dinner seating as well as those who had already seen the other acts. Most of my fan club was back in place, just as noisy as ever. And my duet with Celeste turned into a prolonged and improvised set of mutual putdowns, which the audience loved. The show was going great.

"Intermission" arrived and I rushed back to my dressing room for the quick change. I shut the door behind me and was shocked by what I saw. Someone was sitting in the swivel chair with their back to me. A trespasser! How dare they! Didn't the ship have security guards to keep kooks out of the backstage areas?

"Hey! This is a private room! Get out!"

The person didn't move.

"You're in the wrong room. You have to leave."

Still nothing. Frustrated, I grabbed the chair and spun it around. Jodie Russ was propped in the chair, her face frozen in fright, eyes open and unblinking. She wasn't breathing. One of my show scarves was fastened far too tightly around her neck.

Chapter 7: Dark Moon

I took a step back and gasped. Jodie was dead—no doubt about that. I didn't have to feel for a pulse to deduce that. For a moment, I froze and then my mind raced. What should I do? Call for an ambulance? Call the police? No, wait; I was onboard a moving ship hundreds of miles from shore. Should I contact the captain? Get the ship's doctor? Look for clues? See if the killer was lurking backstage? Pray for Jodie's departed soul?

What I really needed to do was to get my butt back on stage.

My sister's singing wafted through the intercom. She sounded calm and composed, unaware of the crises facing me. She was singing several bars past the point where I should be dressed. The distraction had eaten away precious seconds from my already-tight schedule. The classic cliché "the show must go on" was true—nobody in the house knew about the body, and I needed to finish the show. I couldn't run off to find a security guard or tell the audience to leave just because of a little pesky thing like murder.

I turned the chair so that Jodie faced the wall—I couldn't stand a corpse staring at me. I fumbled around, dropped things, and pulled myself together as best I could. Fortunately, I had extra clean scarves on hand. As I tied the neckpiece (on me, not the body), I couldn't get it to hang right and the ends kept sticking up. By now, Celeste had finished her song. Some applause and then dead silence that only lasted for several seconds but sounded like an eternity. The band began vamping just to make some noise. Celeste, clearly nervous, began asking questions as if I was on stage.

"Sandy isn't here, Celeste," said Frank.

"Where is he?"

She sounded shell-shocked, not only that I was missing in action, but that the people at the tables—the ones who didn't already know—were now well aware of her blindness. During rehearsals with the band, I made a rule that none of the jokes or patter during the show would mention my sister's disability, and no backstage joking about it, not even in fun. Celeste is sensitive about it and wants people to treat her as an equal, not as a charity case.

But for now, I had to get moving and save the show. A quick swallow of water and forget the snacks. When I left the room, I turned the lock in the knob to secure the door behind me. Why did I lock the door? The body wasn't going to walk away. I ran so fast that when I hit the stage, I overshot my mark and almost slid off the front of the platform. I grabbed the mic from the stand. For my sister's benefit, I shouted, "I'm back!" I took a deep breath, tried to clear my mind, and put on a smile.

"What a ship! This barge is so huge I couldn't find my dressing room. I turned left instead of right and ended up on the bridge. The captain wanted me to stay and steer the ship while he came down to watch the show."

Some chuckles from the audience. Hopefully, those who hadn't seen the first show would think this was part of the act. I had no idea what song came next. I was so unnerved I didn't think to look at the set list taped to the floor. I turned to the band. "Now where did we leave off?" Somehow, I got through the rest of the show on cruise control without any major goofs. Despite the midshow mishap, for the curtain call the audience gave us a nice hand—the late hour and all those drinks from the wait staff must have put the guests in a mellow mood.

Celeste, however, wasn't so forgiving. As soon as we got behind the curtain, she shouted, "What happened to you? Why didn't you show up on time? I felt like an idiot out there all alone!"

"Quiet, they can hear us out front."

She lowered her voice just a tad. "Well?"

"I'm sorry; something came up."

"And you're the one telling me to be on time and keep to the script."

I said softly, "There's a dead body in my dressing room."

"That isn't funny."

I grabbed her by the shoulders. "Listen to me, Sis. I'm telling you the truth. While we were doing the show, somebody murdered Jodie Russ and put her body in my dressing room."

"Jodie? Who's Jodie?"

"A woman I met earlier today. She sings in the showroom revue. She's dead."

Her mood changed from anger to panic. "Dead? In your dressing room?"

"I'm afraid so."

Frank peeked out from around the curtain. "Are you two coming out front for autographs?"

I stared at him. "Yeah, right. We'll be there."

"Is something wrong?"

I dropped my hands from my sister's shoulders. "No, no problem."

"I'll go and shut down the instruments."

"Fine, thanks."

Fortunately, he was gone before my sister blurted out, "Ernest, what are we going to do with a dead body?"

"At the moment, nothing. We have to meet the fans. Don't say a word to anyone, got it? As soon as everyone clears the lounge, I'll get help, but for now the fans can't know about this."

"But Ernest, this is terrible!"

"I know. But put on a big smile and act like you're fine. Don't look so worried."

"Is somebody going to come and kill us?"

"No, of course not. We're safe."

Deep down I didn't believe that. Was the body in my dressing room because the killer was after me and Jodie had somehow gotten in the way? Could a serial killer be on the loose, strangling anybody in his path? In my gut I was quaking, but I put on a brave front for the fans. Fortunately, our meet-and-greet didn't last long. Most of the girls in the fan club who had nabbed an autograph after the first show were gone. Only a few of the other guests, as well as the diehards like Bunny, remained.

My fan club president handed me a pencil sketch on a large sheet of drawing paper. "I made this for you, Sandy. I started it during the first show and finished it this time." She'd drawn a remarkably lifelike portrait of Celese and me singing our duet. I'd seen Bunny's artwork before, but this one blew me away.

"Bunny, this is terrific! You've improved tremendously."

"Gosh, I'm just doodling."

"I'll be sure to tell Celeste about this. She'll be pleased."

"It's fun to see how your shows are different. Like when you were late getting back. Did you plan that?"

I can't hide anything from the fans. "I had to deal with something backstage."

She leaned in close to me. "Has there been a murder?"

Bunny had helped me investigate two other crimes recently, but why would she jump to such a conclusion? Or was she just looking for something to do during the long stretches of daytime between the shows?

"I can't talk about it now."

"Sure, I understand. You know you can count on me if you need any help."

She moved out of the way for the next person in line. Now I was rattled. How quickly would the other passengers find out about the death? As soon as I'd signed my last autograph, I ran to my dressing room—and discovered I couldn't open the door.

I knocked on the door of my sister's dressing room. "Sis, it's Ernest. Can I use your phone? My door's locked."

She told me to come in, and I did. Celeste had just started to change clothes. Her skirt was off, but her long slip was still on. "Don't you have a key?"

"No."

"Then why did you lock the door?"

"I wasn't thinking. Look, can I use your phone? I have to talk to someone about you-know-what."

"Okay. Can you please hand me my clothes so I can go in the bathroom and change?"

"Go ahead and get dressed. I have my back to you. I won't look."

On the makeup table was a phone as well as a brochure with the numbers for the various shipboard services. I faced the table, away from Celeste, and dialed.

"Hello, security office," said a calm voice.

What should I say? "I want to report an emergency."

The voice remained unflappable. "What is the nature of your emergency?"

"There's a dead body in my dressing room."

Now the voice sounded confused. "Can you repeat that, sir?"

"My name is Sandy Fairfax. I'm one of the performers on the ship. I'm backstage in the Leo Lounge. A person was murdered in my dressing room. Can you have somebody take care of the situation right away?" A pause at the other end. "This isn't a prank."

Now the voice was a little annoyed. "We'll see who's available. All of the officers are out patrolling the ship." As if pickpockets or casino card sharks were more dangerous than a killer. "Please remain at your location, and someone will be with you shortly."

I thanked him and hung up.

"You can look now, Ernest." Celeste was back in her pantsuit and seated on the stool, slipping on a pair of loafers. I opened the door so I'd spot the security guy when he arrived. But I saw Jackson instead.

"Sandy, there you are," he said. "The door of your dressing room is locked, and I need to take your clothes to the cleaners."

"Right." I was still in my stage costume. "Do you have to do that right now?"

"If you want clean clothes for tomorrow night, yes, I do."

"I can't open the door."

"Why not?"

"It's locked."

"Who locked it? The doors are suppose to stay open during the shows."

"I don't have a key."

"I'll get a passkey from one of the cleaning crew."

I grabbed his arm. "Can you come back in an hour to pick up the clothes?"

Frank appeared in the doorway. "Sandy, Celeste, great show! The band's having drinks in the Gemini Bar to celebrate. Can you join us?"

"Maybe later," I said. "I need to take care of some business first. But tell the guys they did a super job tonight with both shows."

"Thanks, Sandy. They'll appreciate that. By the way, I heard some good comments from the audiences on their way out. They loved the show. Celeste, you were spectacular."

"Thanks." She smiled as he left.

Now if I could just get rid of the other guy. "Jackson, I simply can't let anyone into my dressing room right now."

"What, do you have a dead body in there?" I stared at him and didn't laugh. "That's a joke."

"Jackson, please take Celeste back to her stateroom."

"I'm not staying in my cabin alone." She sounded scared.

I sighed. Now I couldn't get Celeste out of here either. "Jackson, please go. You can take care of the clothes later."

"Can I at least have your microphone?" he said.

"What? Yeah, that." I'd forgotten all about the headset. Jackson helped me get untangled from the wire and battery pack. He scooped my sister's costume off the floor and finally, at long last, bid us good night and cleared out of the room. Celeste and I were the only ones backstage. The silence was eerie. If the killer returned and bumped us off, nobody would know.

"He's gone now. We can talk."

"Ernest, let's go back to the cabin."

"I can't; I have to wait for the security guard."

"I'm scared."

"We're going to be all right, I promise."

An unknown voice said, "Are you Mr. Fairfax?"

I turned to face the open doorway. A middle-aged, African American woman in a navy blue officer's uniform stood in the hall. A small radio transmitter was clipped to the front of her buttoned jacket.

"I'm Sandy Fairfax; who are you?"

"Laytana Marcus, chief security office." Her black hair was pulled back into a bun. Despite her short stature, her composure meant business. "Did you call about a body?"

"Yes, that's right."

She scrunched up her face in puzzlement. "Why is that

name familiar?" Oh boy, here it comes, the reaction when people recognized me. I hoped she wouldn't gush. I wasn't in the mood for fan nostalgia. "Now I remember. My sister had your albums way back a long time ago." It wasn't *that* long ago. "She played those dumb records all the time. Drove me crazy. And I could never watch my favorite TV show because she was always changing the channel to that stupid *Buddy Brave, Boy Sleuth*."

This investigation was off to a rocky start before we'd even started.

I cleared my throat. "This is my sister, Celeste Farmington. We do the show together."

The officer said, "Pleased to meet you, Mrs. Farmington."

"I'm not married," Celeste replied curtly. Sometimes she's also touchy about her lack of a love life. Whereas women threw themselves at me with wild abandon (can't say that I discouraged them), guys took one glance at my sister's disability and ran away.

I explained. "Farmington is my name too. Stanford Ernest Farmington Junior. Sandy Fairfax is my stage name."

Her dark eyes shot me a puzzled look. Now I wished I'd just chucked the deceased overboard and pretended that nothing had happened.

"All of those names—isn't that rather confusing?" said Laytana.

"Not to me, it isn't," I said.

She glanced around the room. "I don't see a body."

"It isn't in here," I said. "It's next door."

"Let's go then." Laytana spoke as if she was just humoring me.

After she stepped in the hall, I said to Celeste, "I'm going to my dressing room. I'd feel better if we stay together."

"You want me to go in there with a dead body?"

"What are you complaining about? You can't see it!"

"What if I trip over it?"

"You won't. It's in a chair."

Laytana stuck her head into the room. "Mr. Fairfax, are you coming?" She sounded impatient.

"Yes, just a minute." I said to my sister. "We need to go now."

Celeste walked to me—she can locate people from the sound of their voice. I gave her my elbow and we left the room. In her nervousness, she dug her fingernails into my arm and squeezed her body against me, but I tolerated the discomfort. Laytana unlocked my dressing room door with a passkey. At the sight of Jodie in the chair, her eyebrows shot up. Maybe now she'd take me seriously.

"Are you sure she's dead?" the officer asked.

"I didn't give her a physical examination, but I'm pretty sure," I said.

The officer circled the chair until she could see Jodie's face. "Is this how you found the body?"

"Yes, just like that."

As Laytana inspected the corpse, Celeste whispered to me, "Where's the body?"

"Sitting in the chair in front of the makeup table," I said. "We're miles away from it. And don't faint on me."

Laytana said, "Mr. Fairfax, have you moved or touched anything in the room?"

"Of course, I have. This is my dressing room. This is where I get ready for the shows."

Laytana gently fingered the scarf around Jodie's neck and then looked at my own neckwear, which I still had on. Why hadn't I removed the blasted thing? "Is this your scarf on the deceased?"

"Yes, I wear those in the show, but anyone could have grabbed that scarf off the clothes rack. They're not hidden."

"Did you know the victim?"

"I met her today, but I don't know her well. Her name is Jodie Russ. And in case you're thinking I'm a suspect, I have an alibi. I was on stage doing a concert. I have a roomful of eyewitnesses."

"What time was this show?"

"I went on at ten-thirty. I had people in the room before then, and they can testify that the body wasn't here at that time. I came back here at eleven o'clock. That's when I found her. So whoever killed Jodie did so between ten-thirty and eleven."

"The show ended at eleven?"

"No, eleven-thirty. At eleven I leave the stage long enough for a costume change."

"How long were you in the room?"

"About three, four minutes."

Celeste said, "You took longer than that." She was not helping my case.

Laytana said to my sister, "Ma'am, how long was he off stage?"

"It seemed like a long time. I'd finished my song, and everyone was waiting for him to get back"

I felt like strangling Celeste.

Laytana eyed me. "While you were in this room with your costume change, did you see or hear anyone during that time?"

"No, during the show everyone's out front."

"You didn't see the killer arrive or leave?"

The exhaustion of doing two shows had caught up with me. I wanted to hit the sack instead of standing here, playing twenty questions about a murder. "If I had, don't you think I would have given you a description?"

The officer crossed her arms. "Miss Farmington, did you see or hear anything suspicious before or during the concert?"

Celeste snapped out her words. "No, I didn't *see* anything because I'm *blind.*"

"Begging your pardon, ma'am. I'm just trying to get the facts."

I said, "Can you please move Jodie out of the room so I can shower and get dressed?"

"I'm afraid you can't use this room until we've had a chance to look for evidence."

"May I at least take my clothes?"

"We need to leave everything exactly the way it is. In two days we'll dock at Key West. I'll contact the authorities and see if they can send a technician. In the meantime, this room is off limits."

"I have two shows tomorrow night. What do I use for a dressing room?"

"What's wrong with using your stateroom? That's where you get dressed in the morning. Now if you'll excuse me, I need to contact the captain."

"The band is going to ask why I'm not using my dressing room."

"Tell them we found mold or the toilet overflowed or a circuit blew. You're a creative man, Mr. Fairfax. You can think of something to say."

"But you're not canceling the shows?"

"Of course not," said Laytana. "The guests are here to enjoy themselves. We'll stick to the scheduled programming so's not to cause an alarm. That means the two of you are not to discuss this matter with anyone—not the crew, not the passengers. We don't want to start a panic."

"You're going to investigate this, right?" I said, "and not just hide the body?"

Laytana glared at me. "One thing you should know, Mr. Fairfax, is that I cannot stand amateur sleuths. They hinder more than they help. Civilians watch a few episodes of *Law and Order* on TV and think they can solve a case with a few crackpot ideas. I've had my share of passengers who have had their valuables stolen and then try to tell me who did it. They were wrong every time. The best thing the two of you can do is not to interfere. Do I make myself clear?"

"Absolutely."

Celeste pulled on my arm. "Ernest, let's get out of here."

"That's a very wise idea, young lady." Laytana switched on her radio to call the captain, the signal that she was finished talking with us.

I was ready to leave anyway. Even though I was still awake, the sight of Jodie in that chair gave me nightmares. I glanced at the wall clock—twelve-thirty. What a way to end my first day at sea. Celeste and I were in no mood to party with the band, so we headed for our cabins. For privacy we took the crew stairs, which were off-limits to the passengers. I was still in my stage costume, so I got some odd looks from the crewmembers passing by.

In my room, I found my bedcovers pulled down and one of the bath towels, cleverly folded into the shape of an animal, resting atop the bed. If I weren't so upset about the murder, I would have enjoyed the sight. In the safety and comfort of our rooms, I showered and put on my jammies and bathrobe. Celeste then met me in my suite. She'd changed into a lounging caftan. Since she couldn't see the towel animal on her bed, she had sat on it, so I gave her mine. I said I was going to call room service for a late dinner. Celeste was still too shaken to eat, but she wanted her usual brandy—I'm sure she needed it to recoup from the shock. I invited her to share a large loaded pizza with me.

She frowned. "Pizza at this hour? What about your diet?"

"The way I feel right now, I need either comfort food or booze, and food won't get me drunk. I'll work off the calories in the morning. And you need to eat too."

Celeste reluctantly agreed to share a slice or two of pizza. I phoned in the order, and while we waited we sat in the chairs to talk.

"How are you holding up?" I asked.

"I'm still shaking. You seemed pretty calm when you were talking to that cop."

"I'm a good actor. Anyway, this isn't the first dead body I've seen." I briefed her on the two recent incidents where I had unwittingly witnessed the death of two other murder victims—and found their killers. When I finished my tale, the food arrived. I set the food and drinks—O'Doul's for me—on the table. But before we could dig in, someone knocked at the door.

Celeste said, "Is that the murderer?"

"Of course not. Nobody knows we're here." When I embarked, I had given orders to the crew not to give out our phone or room numbers to anyone, especially not to the fan club. But did someone follow without us knowing? I used the peephole in the door and sighed in relief.

"It's only Jackson." I opened the door. I'd given my location to Jackson and Frank in case we needed to communicate about the shows.

"Hi, Sandy. Hello, Celeste. I'm sorry if I woke you."

"No, no, we're still up. What can I do for you?"

"I came to pick up your costume for the cleaners."

After I'd showered in the suite, I'd left the clothes in a heap on the bathroom floor. "How did you know I had it in here?"

"The security officer said you had gone to your cabin."

"You mean Laytana? When did you meet her?"

"Just now. I went back to your dressing room for the clothes and I saw—"

I grabbed Jackson's arm, pulled him into the room, and shut the door. "What did you see?"

"The captain was there, and so was the ship's doctor. The ship's photographer was taking a ton of pictures around the room. A couple of crewmen were putting something on a stretcher. When I asked what was going on, the officer told me to get lost."

"I'm not supposed to tell anyone, but you deserve to know. During the second show, when I left for my costume change, I found a dead body in my dressing room. That's why I was late getting back on stage."

Jackson's eyes went wide. "A dead body?"

I nodded. "Jodie Russ, a singer with the revue."

"How did a body get into your dressing room?"

"That's what I'd like to know."

"That's terrible. Someone just walked into your dressing room and died?"

"No, she was murdered. Tell you what, Jackson. Tell the band I want to meet with them tomorrow—I mean today— in the lounge at nine-thirty. I'll tell them what happened. But I have to swear you and the guys to secrecy. We can't discuss this with anyone."

"Sure, Sandy, I understand. Nine-thirty it is. And where are your dirty clothes?"

That's what made Jackson such a good roadie—he was a man with a mission. I fetched the clothes for him. He bid us goodnight and left. I finally sat down with the pizza, which, fortunately, was still warm enough to eat. As we munched, we talked about—what else—the murder. Now that Celeste was away from the scene of the crime, she was quite chatty—or maybe it was just nerves.

"The killer used one of your scarves to kill her?" she asked. "That's mean."

"That's how it appears, but it doesn't make sense. My scarves are made of thin material. I don't see how something that flimsy can choke a person to death."

"Maybe Jodie was already dead, and the murderer added

the scarf to frame you."

"Sis, you read too many detective novels."

"But doesn't that make sense? Your scarf, your dressing room."

"Why would the killer go to the trouble of framing anyone? Why not just throw the body overboard?"

"Maybe somebody doesn't like you."

"Who would that be? I don't know anyone on this ship except you, the fan club and the band."

"What about the people at your dinner table?"

I'd forgotten about them. I described my interesting dinner companions.

"The murderer has to be one of them," Celeste said. "In mystery books, the killer is always someone who knows the victim well."

"Knock it off."

"The performers are the only ones who have access to the crew hallway. That must be how the killer got in and out of your dressing room without the passengers seeing him."

"Could have been a passenger." I tore off another slice of pizza topped with pepperoni and sausage. "The door to the crew hallway isn't locked, and there's no guard posted. Anyone could have slipped in. Besides, your theory has a big flaw."

She talked between bites of pizza. "What's that?"

"If Jodie was killed between ten-thirty and eleven, all the performers were doing their shows. Each one has an alibi."

"You're just trying to confuse me."

By now, we'd demolished most of the pizza, and we were both too worn out to continue the conversation. We said our goodnights, and Celeste carried her brandy into her suite. I set the tray of dirty dishes in the hallway for pickup. I couldn't sleep, so I took the O'Doul's and sat in a lounge chair on my cabin's private balcony. A million stars and a full moon shone in the clear night sky. The water softly lapped against the hull as the ship plowed onward. I breathed in the clean sea air. From the Lido Deck above came the faint sounds of merrymakers and recorded music. How could anyone party when there'd been a murder? I stared at the black water and wondered who indeed had killed Jodie—and whether he'd strike again.

TUESDAY: At Sea
Chapter 8: Too Much Monkey Business

Bright and early—that is, early for me the day after a late show—I was up at seven a.m. Actually, the clatter of the food carts outside my door woke me up. Why can't people go to the dining room for breakfast? Then an alarm went off in the hallway for a test drill among the crew. Doesn't anyone sleep in on this ship? Since I was too wound up to doze off again, I figured I might as well get up. Celeste was still snoozing, so I threw on shorts, a shirt and flip-flops, grabbed my gym bag, and headed for the Recreation Deck, the topmost level just above the Lido Deck.

At the gym, I changed into my sweats and put in a hardy workout not only to keep my figure, but also to work off my frustration at how this cruise was shaping up. Of all the dressing rooms onboard this ship, how did Jodie's body end up in mine? And if she was dead at eleven o'clock last night, she couldn't have performed in the revue's second show. Didn't anyone—particularly the audience—notice her absence? The corpse was in stage makeup and clad in tights and a brightly colored sequined dance outfit, so apparently at the time of Jodie's demise she had either just finished her number or was ready to go onstage. Laytana wasn't interested in my theories, so I better see for myself how the revue carried on last night without its diva.

I finished exercising in about an hour. I put on my swimsuit, stuffed my sweats and street clothes into the gym bag, and headed down a flight of stairs to the Lido Deck. A few hardy souls jogged along the track that circled the perimeter of the deck, but most of the passengers were still in their cabins, sleeping off their late-night parties. Now would be a great time to get in a few laps while the pool was empty of obnoxious kids and the fans. I wanted to lose a few more pounds before the fans trained their cameras on me wearing naught but a swimsuit. After a refreshing dip, I dried off with a ship's towel and put on my shirt but didn't button it. I leaned against the railing for a few moments to take in the bright sky, gentle breeze and quiet morning. The peace and serenity didn't last long.

"Ernest! Ernest Farmington!"

Only my family and close friends used my given name. I turned around. A gorgeous brunette just a tad younger than myself ran toward me. One ring-laden hand waved at me, and the other clutched a Bloody Mary. The breeze whipped up the sleeves of her purple muumuu. Few people drank this early in the morning, but this woman could pack it away all night. I should know—I used to guzzle right along with her. She caught up with me and stretched her full lips into a fetching smile.

"Ernest! Fancy meeting you here! What serendipity!"

"Hello, Helen," I said with a pronounced lack of sincerity. I nodded at her glass. "Didn't take you long to find the bar. Or did you camp there all night?"

"Oooooo, look who got up on the wrong side of the porthole this morning. Is that any way to greet an old friend?"

"An old *ex*-girlfriend. As I recall, we broke up several months ago. Don't you remember moving out of my house, or do you have amnesia?"

She took a swig of her drink and pouted. "You *kicked* me out."

"That's because you wouldn't leave when I asked you nicely."

"Putting me out like a cat, alone and homeless on the mean streets of L.A."

"You were never homeless. You took the money you stole out of my dresser and got your own apartment. And then the tabloids paid you a fortune for blabbing your hot story of what it was like bedding down with Buddy Brave."

"A girl's gotta make a living."

"I wouldn't have minded so much if you'd at least told the truth."

"Don't start the day as a sourpuss. You never tolerated mornings well." Helen Wheeler seized my arm with her free hand. I was going to pry off her hand, until I considered what she might want to grab next. She swished her Bloody Mary back and forth. "Have a drink with me and we can talk about old times. Or new times. Or no time at all." She threw back her long, thick hair and laughed.

"I don't drink anymore."

"Now that doesn't sound like the Ernest I know."

"You're right. That jerk isn't around anymore. The new, improved Ernest wants you to leave him alone."

She gave me an exaggerated pout. "Now, Ernest, after all the money I spent just to be near you again—"

"You came on this cruise just to stalk me?"

"You make it sound so terrible."

"It is. Helen, I don't want to cause a scene, but you can't be bothering me. We're through, finished, over and out. There are plenty of other poor souls onboard this ship for you to pester. Now if you'll excuse me—" I levered her fingers from my arm. "I have to go check on Celeste."

"Celeste? Is that your new girlfriend?"

"No. My sister."

"I'd love to meet her."

"If you get within thirty yards of her, I'll—"

"Do what? Get another restraining order? But you can't 'cause we're at sea. Ha, ha." I picked up my gym bag and started walking away—she followed. "I was going to see your show last night, but I was in my cabin with an upset tummy. But I saw the doctor this morning, and he fixed me right up."

"The doctor? Is the doctor here?" What luck. If this were the same physician who was at the crime scene last night, maybe he'd found some clues on the body. The doctor already knew about the death, so I could talk to him freely despite Laytana's warning.

"Why do you want the doctor? Are you sick?"

"Yes, I'm sick of you. Now go away, Helen, before I get mad."

She shoved her body against my chest, pressing my back against the railing. "Are you gonna kill me like you did that singer?"

My mind shorted out. I glanced around to see if anyone was listening. I whispered, "How do you know about that?"

She looked at her glass and then took a drink. "Oh, I hear things."

"Did you bribe some spineless crewmember into talking?"

"Really, Ernest."

"I didn't kill anybody, and I'd be grateful if you wouldn't spread rumors about—that."

"*How* grateful?"

"Goodbye, Helen."

I pushed her aside and ran across the deck as fast as my flip-flops could take me. I ducked into the crew stairwell, hoping Helen had the decency not to follow. I headed down two flights for the Leo Lounge to meet with my band. What was I going to do about my former flame? I couldn't spend the week looking over my shoulder to see if she was on my tail. However, the ship was large, and maybe I could lose her. She never had a good sense of direction, and the bars would distract her. Who was I fooling? Helen wouldn't quit until she had me cornered.

When I arrived at the lounge, I popped into my sister's dressing room long enough to button my shirt and change from the swimsuit into my shorts. Jackson, Frank and the band members were waiting, seated in the audience chairs. Some of the musicians looked bedraggled after having celebrated deep into the night. I didn't mind—they had nothing to do until the show tonight. I'd rather they worked off steam through a few beers than in trashing their cabins or other rock star tomfoolery (for the record, during my heyday I never wrecked a hotel room or otherwise misbehaved on tour. After working so hard during a concert, I was too pooped to party).

I told Jackson to fetch coffee for everyone. Once we all had some caffeine in our systems, I told them about finding the body last night. I warned them that Laytana might question them, and they had to be honest— although what could they say? They were in the lounge during the whole affair, and the instruments were cranked up so loud they couldn't hear a bomb going off backstage. They assured me that none of them knew the victim. I said I'd keep them posted if and when I heard any updates about the investigation. They seemed relieved when I assured them the shows would continue. Then we discussed the concerts from last night and smoothed out a couple of rough spots. When I dismissed the guys, they wandered backstage to peek at my dressing room, which was locked and had a hand-printed sign taped to the door that read "Keep Out."

I returned to my stateroom. After a shower, shave, and a change into a tee shirt and clean shorts, I knocked lightly on the connecting door. By now, Celeste was awake. I found her seated and brushing her hair. She wore slacks, sneakers, socks and a short-sleeve blouse.

"Did you sleep well?" I asked.

"No. The ship was rocking, and the bed was hard, and I

couldn't stop thinking about the murder."

"So other than that, you're all right? Hey, I'm famished. Want to have breakfast with me?"

"I was going to call room service."

"Let's go up on the Lido Deck for the buffet. It's too nice a day to stay cooped up in the rooms."

"But that killer's out there."

"It's broad daylight with plenty of people around. We'll be safe out in the open. C'mon, Sis, it'll do you good to get around."

"I don't know. I still feel a little queasy."

"Tell you what. We'll got to the infirmary and pick up some more Dramamine." This would give me a good excuse to stop by the ship's hospital and grill the doctor on what he knew about the murder. "It's in the contract you signed with the cruise line. You're required to get out of your room for at least five hours a day."

"My contact doesn't say that."

"How do you know? Did you read it?"

"Marshall read it to me."

"And you trust him?"

"More than I trust you."

I said the doctor wouldn't prescribe any Dramamine unless the patient was there in person. I was probably lying, but I wanted to spring her from her self-imposed exile. She finally relented. Celeste put on her fanny pack and dark glasses and picked up her folding cane, which was made up of several thin metal tubes with a cord running through them. With a flick of her wrist, the device unfolded into a long white cane. She hated using the cane because she felt it made people stare at her even more, but being in an unfamiliar place with strangers around, she had no choice. I offered to guide her but she said, no, she'd like to try this on her own as long as I stayed close. We headed for the elevator with me stuck like glue to her side, and Celeste making small sweeps of the cane to check the path ahead. She didn't have to worry about collisions—as soon as the passengers saw the cane, they stepped aside and let us pass.

At the infirmary, we met Dr. John Carpenter. Celeste folded her cane, and the nurse on duty gave her a Dramamine patch to wear behind her ear. After the nurse went into another room to check on a bed-ridden patient, I told the doctor about my experience last night and asked if he knew anything about Jodie's body.

He had no compunctions talking about it. "We had quite a discussion on how best to preserve the body until we reached Key West. Since the deceased is an American citizen, we'll be releasing the body to the authorities in Florida. The food service director said we'd be breaking every sanitation law on the planet if we kept a human body in the galley. That wasn't an option anyway, since at the start of a cruise the freezers are full."

"So what did you do?" I asked.

"Down in a lower deck, the crew filled a large metal bin with ice to store the body. They have orders to replace the ice as it melts. Not very dignified, I'm afraid, but it should do the job."

"Sounds like the humane thing to do," I said. "Doc, did you see anything strange or unusual about the body?"

"You mean did I examine it? Mind you, I'm not a forensic scientist, and I don't have an extensive laboratory here. But I did notice something about the ligature mark."

"You mean the—" I drew my finger around my neck.

"Exactly. I didn't see any bruises that would indicate she was choked by hand. What I noticed was a thin, deep groove, possibly caused by a thin rope."

"Would a scarf leave a mark like that?"

"Doubtful, but as I said, I'm not an expert in post-mortem cases. Fortunately, we don't have many deaths aboard ship. I've only handled one in my time with the cruise line, an elderly gentleman who suffered a heart attack by natural causes. By the way, the police will want to keep that scarf as evidence."

"That's fine. I don't want it back."

"Oh, another thing. I found some dirt on the victim's clothing. Off the top of my head, I might surmise that the body had been on the floor and then placed in the chair. The crew does a topnotch job of keeping the ship clean, but sometimes dust builds up on floors that don't see a great deal of foot traffic, such as down in the engine rooms."

"So, she was killed while she was standing and then she fell to the ground?" Celeste said. Apparently she was losing her aversion to discussing death.

"But the floor of my dressing room was clean," I said. "When I arrived last night, the floor had just been swept. Besides, if Jodie had fallen to the floor, why didn't the killer just leave her there? Picking her up would take time, and the murderer would probably want to get out of my room pronto."

Before the doctor could reply, Laytana entered the room—just what I needed to spice up my day. She eyed me. "What are you doing here?" From the tone of her voice, she was in dire need of a morning cup of coffee.

"I wasn't aware certain rooms onboard the ship were off limits," I said.

Celeste came to my rescue. "I needed some Dramamine. I have a terrible problem with motion sickness."

"Very well," the officer said. "If you have your medicine, you may leave. I need to talk with the doctor privately."

"About a medical condition or the body?" I said.

"Mr. Fairfax, I told you before that I don't need you getting in the way of our investigation."

"But I can help. The suspects might open up to me more than they would to the police."

"Suspects? You're already accusing people without evidence?"

"The doctor said the body might have been moved after the murder. If I were you, I'd examine the body closely and start looking for clues."

"My job aboard this ship is to keep the passengers and their possessions safe and secure. Your job, Mr. Fairfax, is to entertain said passengers twice each night. Do not confuse our job descriptions. I would hate to confine the two of you to your cabins for the duration of this trip—but I will if I have to. Is that understood?"

"Perfectly." I snapped off the word with as much hostility as I could muster. "If you'll excuse us, Celeste and I would like to take advantage of the breakfast buffet while we're still free to roam around."

I grabbed my sister by her upper arm—something I rarely do, except in emergencies—and ushered her into the corridor. Once there, she pulled away from my grip and snapped her cane into place.

She said, "You should have asked the doctor to treat your foot-in-mouth disease."

"Laytana is the one who needs a dose of good manners and common sense. How is she going to find a killer among a thousand people if she doesn't have an inside man like myself helping out?"

"If you're not careful, she'll kick us off the ship just for spite. While it's still moving."

"If she does, I'd sue the cruise line for breach of contract."

"I think you need some breakfast to calm you down."

Sounded like a plan to me. By this time of day, the Lido Deck was starting to fill up with people. I found a pair of unoccupied lounge chairs away from the pool and in some shade where we wouldn't be bothered. The Lido Deck had a buffet open until late at night for those who wanted a faster, more casual eating experience than the dining room. After a short wait in line, I grabbed a tray and filled it with enough food to share between the two of us: coffee, juice, eggs and bacon, fresh fruit and toasted English muffins with jam. Normally, I didn't eat this much so early in the day, but the sea air and my workout must have given me an appetite.

As we ate, I warned Celeste about Helen. "If she bothers you, call me on your two-way radio. Don't talk to her. Don't tell her anything about yourself."

"Ernest, I can handle myself around your old mistakes. And I don't need you running to my rescue like I'm a helpless damsel."

"You don't know Helen. She's sly, cunning, evil, a liar—"

"So why did you ever hook up with her?"

"At the time, we had something in common. Booze." I stopped chewing on my English muffin. Talking about Helen triggered a thought. "What if Helen killed Jodie and put her in my room for revenge?"

"That's crazy. Why would she hurt Jodie?"

"Helen's unbalanced. She's nuts. Maybe she went looking for a random victim, and Jodie got in the way. Or perhaps she saw me talking to Jodie and thought we had a thing going."

Celeste put her fork down. "What did Jodie say to you?"

"Nothing."

"Maybe she said something that—"

"Jodie made fun of you for being blind." Celeste's face scrunched up as if she might cry. "I'm sorry. I wasn't going to tell you."

She took a deep breath. "It's okay. She isn't the first one." Celeste ate a forkful of eggs. "If Jodie's body was moved, maybe she was killed earlier in the day."

"And the killer hung onto the body until eleven o'clock?

If I had a corpse, I'd dump it as soon as possible."

"But it makes sense, Ernest. Think about it. Early in the evening, the ship is crowded. People are moving all over the place. They're going to the dining room, the casino, the venues. After ten-thirty the dining room is closed, and people are settled for the evening. The hallway is clear. The killer could move the body without being seen."

"Okay, I'll buy that. But the big question is: where did the killer store the body? Jodie was alive and well at six-twenty when I left the dining room. That means she might have been dead for almost five hours before I found her. The killer couldn't hide the body in a cabin, because that's the time when the crew pulls down the beds."

Just then, a crewmember carrying a tray of clean glassware passed me.

"Excuse me!" I said.

He stopped. "Yes, sir?"

"Did the revue go on last night? You know, the one in the Sagittarius Showroom?"

"Of course, sir."

"It wasn't cancelled?"

"Oh, no, sir. It's very popular and always well attended."

"Both shows ran last night at the scheduled time?"

"Yes, sir."

"Will it be on tonight as well?"

"Yes, sir. You can see it any night this week except Friday. I'm sure you'll enjoy it."

"I'm sure I would. Thanks for your time."

After he left, I placed my tray on the deck. "Now that's a mystery. If Jodie's the lead singer in the show, how did it go on without her? Even if she was still alive for the first show, she was a definite no-show at ten-thirty."

Chapter 9: Girls! Girls! Girls!

Before I could ponder this predicament further, a beguiling creature slinked up beside me: a willowy, young lady dressed in a long colorful peasant skirt. She had a kerchief tied around her head and wore a white blouse with the sleeves pulled down below her lovely tanned shoulders. She was loaded with enough costume jewelry to stock a department store—long necklaces, bracelets, jingly earrings and even bells on her sandals. Her makeup was extreme though—blood-red lipstick and so much cheek rouge that I thought she had a fever.

Celeste, of course, heard the jingly baubles. "Who's that?"

"I'm not sure, but she's headed our way."

The woman sat on the edge of my lounger and ran her long fingers through my hair—I made no effort to stop her.

"Welcome aboard zee Zodiac." She spoke in a pseudo-Eastern European accent as thick as a bowl of borsch. "I am Madam Balorinsky, teller of fortunes and reader of palms. I cast horoscopes as well. Kind sir, what is your date of birth?"

"December 25, 1955."

That's right, I'm a Christmas baby, best present my parents ever received. When I was a kid, I got in big trouble during Sunday School when the teacher asked whose birthday we celebrated on Christmas, and I said, "Mine!" The holiday birthday didn't bother me because I got more presents that day than my siblings. Instead of the traditional holiday desserts for Christmas dinner, though, my family served a birthday cake.

"Ah ha!" said the woman. "Capricorn, an earth sign. You are strong, independent, patient, loyal and responsible."

Celeste giggled. "Are you sure that's a Capricorn?"

"Hush!" To Madam, I said, "Please go on."

"You are inquisitive, perhaps too much so. You ask questions for which there are no answers. I see fear and anxiety in your eyes. Perhaps you've had a recent close call with danger—or death?"

Did Madam know something about Jodie's death? "You're very perceptive."

"Madam sees all and knows all."

Celeste put her tray on the floor and stuck out her hand. "Hey, read my palm."

Madam took Celeste's hand. She leaned in and traced her fingers along the creases. "Your life line takes an abrupt turn. You must be careful in the days ahead. Someone may seek to do you harm. Your love line—ah, that's very interesting."

"Interesting? What's interesting about it?"

"Someone new will enter your life very soon. Someone whom you will love very much. But they will not be at all what you expected."

I smiled. "Sis, I didn't know you were dating."

She looked surprised. "I'm not."

As Madam babbled on about my sister's future, I studied the woman's face. Something about the seer seemed familiar.

"You're Nessie, aren't you?" I said. "The magician's daughter?"

She nodded, and dropped Celeste's hand.

"Why the act?"

Nessie used her normal voice. "I do 'Madam' to entertain the passengers during the day. It brings in some extra tips. It's fun and helps to pass the time when I'm not on stage. I can talk to real people, not those silly performers."

"I'm sorry I blew your cover. You do it very well. By the way, this is my sister, Celeste Farmington. She's in the show with me."

"How do you do?" Nessie shook the hand she had just "read." "I'm Nessie Stevenford. My father and I are magicians. I didn't see you at dinner last night."

"I was at the salon," Celeste said. "Can you really read minds and tell fortunes?"

"In a way. I've tested high for extra-sensory perception."

"No, she can't, Sis. It's an act, just like her magic show." Some cobwebs began clearing out of my dense mind. "Nessie, you and your dad do your act during the Starlight Ocean Revue, is that right?"

"Yes. Father and I are in the second half of the show, after the opening musical number and the juggler."

"Did Jodie Russ perform last night during the eight-forty-five show?"

"I assume so. Why?"

"Don't you know?"

"Father and I are occupied when we're off stage. We both need to stay focused on what we do. Watching the other acts distracts us."

"Did you see Jodie backstage before or after shows last night?"

"No. We keep the magic props in a separate area away from the dressing rooms. Before the show, we test the equipment, and afterward we put it away. Between the shows, father and I don't socialize with the other performers." She gave me a look. "This is about Jodie's disappearance, isn't it?"

"Does everyone on the ship know about that?"

"The people in the revue do. After the first show, Hugh came to me and—"

"Hugh? Who's that?"

"Hugh Adams, the stage manager. He asked if I'd seen Jodie, and I said no. After the second show, I heard that she never showed up."

"How did the revue go on?"

"We used Jodie's understudy."

Why didn't I think of that?

Celeste jumped in. "Did you find out what happened to Jodie?"

Nessie shrugged those beautiful shoulders. "Doesn't matter now. Hugh doesn't take kindly to performers who play hooky. I doubt he'd let her back in the show even if she begged."

I said, "Is it possible that Jodie met with foul play?"

Nessie said, "If someone wanted to hurt Jodie, my guess would be Aaron."

"The ventriloquist?" I asked. "Why is that?"

"Once upon a time they were married." After Nessie dropped that bombshell, she stood up. "If you'll excuse me, I need to mingle with the other guests. I'm not supposed to linger too long with any one person."

"Of course, didn't mean to hold up your work. Thank you, Madam. That was most illuminating."

She gave an exaggerated bow and resumed her fake accent. "Of course. Madam Balorinsky is always right." She gave me a wink and slithered away. Within minutes, she had buttonholed another victim at the buffet counter, scrutinizing the palm of a shirtless man with a waistline spilling over the top of his shorts.

I turned my attention to Celeste. "Do you think she knows about the murder?"

"I couldn't tell. She's a hard one to read."

"Nessie's an actor. She knows how to hide her feelings.

I wonder if she was telling the truth about Jodie and Aaron. I can't picture those two together."

"It's usually the spouse who commits murder. I heard it on the TV news. That's a fact."

I stood up and stretched. The tropical sun was making me drowsy. "I need to get moving. If I stay here any longer without sunscreen, I'll be as red as the lobster at dinner."

Celeste had finished eating, so we headed for the elevator. The cab door opened and, by an amazing coincidence, Cinnamon stepped out.

"Sandy!" She moved to the side to let the other passengers out of the elevator. "You're just the man I wanted to see. Oh, and hello, Celeste."

"Hi, Cinnamon." Celeste recognized her voice.

"What can I do for you?" I said.

"We need to work on the dances, remember?" Cinnamon looked yummy in a halter-top, shorts, a floppy-brim hat and sandals that laced up her ankle.

The choreographer and I agreed to meet for a rehearsal in the Leo Lounge in an hour. That would give her time for breakfast on the Lido Deck and me a chance to sleuth around. Celeste wanted to return to her cabin for some rest and reading her books on tape—too much socializing and dealing with strange environments wore her out.

After dropping Celeste off at her cabin, I made my way to the crew passageway behind the Sagittarius Showroom. I wondered how I'd get in—the backstage area might be locked—but fortunately I found a dressing room open. A man—probably late thirties, in a striped long-sleeved shirt, tennis shoes, khakis and suspenders—was packing items into a trunk.

"Excuse me; I'm looking for Hugh Adams."

The man stopped what he was doing. "You've found him. Say, you're Sandy Fairfax. I heard you were on the ship. Wish I could catch your act. I loved your TV show."

"Thank you."

"If you're interested in doing another cruise, I can work you into the revue. I see you as Neptune and the dancers as your mermaids."

The idea of being surrounded by a bevy of lovely young ladies in bikinis appealed to me, but for now I had to stay on target. "I was supposed to meet Jodie Russ for coffee this morning, but I hear she's missing."

"Missing? You mean she's dead!"

I feigned surprise. "Dead? I don't believe it."

"The security chief informed me this morning. How do you like that! We barely leave port, and I lose a performer."

"What did she die of?"

"Laytana didn't say. Sounds fishy though. Sometimes Jodie drank too much, but otherwise she was strong as an ox. So now I'm stuck clearing out her things."

"Can I help?" Maybe I could find a clue somewhere among her effects.

"You sure you don't mind?"

"I'd be happy to help out."

Hugh scooted an empty trunk along the floor in my direction. "Okay, start with the closet. Jodie had a small cabin, so she stashed some of her belongings in here. I don't know why she needed so many clothes for a five-day cruise."

As we talked, I took the items off the hangers, folded and stowed them in the trunk. The late diva owned a mountain of designer-label slacks, tops and dinner dresses, not to mention a pair of shoes for every outfit.

"So what happened last night?" I spoke casually so I wouldn't sound like an interrogator. "I saw Jodie at dinner, and she seemed fine. Then I heard she wasn't here for the second show."

"You got that right, mister. The rule is once the performers sign in for the night, they stay put. There isn't enough time between shows for them to wander around the ship and for me to herd them back. If there's an emergency, they can leave only if they check with me first and tell me where they're going. Jodie never talked to me—she just disappeared. Pulled off a better vanishing act than the magician. I called her room, but she didn't answer. I even checked with the bars, but nobody had seen her. At ten-twenty, I had no choice but to put in the understudy."

"Jodie never showed up after ten-twenty?"

"Wouldn't matter if she did. In my book, a late arrival is the same as a no-show. I'm not holding the curtain for irresponsible performers."

"But she was here until the first show ended at, when?"

"The revue runs a full sixty minutes. Wait, I think Jodie was missing from the company bow. At the finale, all of the acts take a group bow, but she wasn't on her mark. At the time I didn't think about it, because I was busy running cues."

"How could she leave before the show ended?"

"She's only on at the top of the show. We open with a big song and dance number—Jodie was the principal singer—and then we run some of the specialty acts and another set piece with a different singer."

So Jodie might have been murdered as early as nine o'clock.

Hugh came over to help me untangle the endless mounds of shoes. Much of the footwear looked barely used.

"She left enough clothes to stock your whole wardrobe department," I commented.

"I wired Jodie's parents and asked if I can donate some of these outfits to the other girls. They're young and can't afford high-end clothes like these." He scrutinized an especially gaudy set of high heels. "How did she buy all of this on her salary? She must have been working some good gigs on land between cruises."

"I heard that Jodie wasn't Miss Congeniality."

"Great singer, abrasive personality. When you're in tight quarters like these, you need a cast that gets along." He stopped packing and stared at me. "Are you suggesting that someone killed Jodie?"

"No, not really. Just seems peculiar, a healthy woman suddenly dies—"

"If she met with foul play, nobody in the revue is guilty. We all have airtight alibis. We were either onstage or backstage from eight o'clock to nearly midnight. I'll vouch for every performer and technician."

A lovely young lady skipped into the room. She was carrying a suitcase, which she dropped beside the closet. She opened the luggage, pulled out some clothes, grabbed the closet hangers and began hanging up her own things. Then she noticed me.

"Who are you?" She sounded suspicious and a tad irked.

"He's all right, Mindy," said Hugh. "It's Sandy Fairfax, one of the other performers."

"How do you do?" I said.

She grabbed the silver locket hanging around her neck and absently swung it back and forth as she talked. "I didn't see you in the revue last night."

"I have my own show in the Leo Lounge."

"And what is it that you do?"

So much for fame and fortune. She probably wasn't born yet when I hit my stride years ago but, really, didn't she ever see my TV show in syndication or listen to oldies radio?

I straightened up and said proudly, "I sing."

"How nice." She didn't sound impressed. "Hugh, love, can you help me move my stuff in here?"

"Give me a few minutes," Hugh said. "I need to clear out Jodie's clothes first so we don't get your things mixed up with hers."

"Don't worry about that. I don't want any of her ugly old rags."

"What happened to the other charm on your necklace?"

She looked at said piece of jewelry. "I dunno. I guess it fell off."

"Quit yanking on it or you'll lose the other one. Those charms are expensive."

I said to the girl, "Are you the understudy?"

She grinned broadly. "Not anymore!"

Hugh gave her a swat on that tight little tush. "Run along, Mindy; I'll catch up with you later." He passionately kissed her on the mouth. She giggled and ran out of the room.

No surprise that Hugh wasn't heartbroken over Jodie's absence. Thanks to the diva's death, Hugh's main squeeze had been promoted to queen bee. Seemed like both of them had a good reason for wanting Jodie off the ship. As for alibis, I'm sure Hugh wouldn't mind letting Mindy slip away from the showroom long enough to snuff out a competitor. Plus, nobody was keeping tabs on Hugh's location during the shows.

Since he was occupied with cleaning out the closet, I turned my attention to the makeup table. I opened the top drawer and found enough eye shadow, lipstick, combs, packets of false eyelashes and other beauty gear to keep the Avon Company in business for years. Unless I'm doing my own makeup for a show, I don't like dealing with this stuff, so I closed the top drawer and decided to see if the rest of the table had something more interesting in it. I pulled on the handle of the second drawer, but it didn't budge.

"Hugh, are these drawers locked?"

"No, why?"

"This one's stuck."

On a count of three, we both grabbed and pulled the handle. The drawer flew out, spilling its contents across the floor. Hugh knelt down and began picking up various papers, small notebooks and address books. I put my hand on the bottom of the drawer to keep from dropping it. I felt something. I turned the drawer over, bottom side up. A manila envelope was duct-taped on the bottom.

"Hugh, look at this."

He sat on his knees and looked up. "That's odd. I've never seen that before."

"Why would she hide something here? If there are important papers, she could have put them in her room safe."

While Hugh finished cleaning up the paper goods on the floor, I set the drawer upside down on the makeup table and peeled off the envelope. I used one of Jodie's metal nail files to rip open the package. I removed the contents and then wished I hadn't. The envelope held several eight-by-ten color photos of a distinguished middle-age man and Jodie in what looked like one of the ship's expensive suites, both of them au natural and doing what comes naturally.

Chapter 10: Puppet On A String

Hugh stood up and reached for the photos. "What is it?"

I pressed the glossies against my chest so he couldn't see them. "Ah, nothing, nothing at all."

"If it's important papers, I need to give them to Jodie's parents."

"Trust me, they don't want this."

With the envelope and photos in hand, I dashed out of the dressing room before he could grab the pictures from me. I headed for my stateroom, running up the crew stairs two at a time and blushing all the way. I had to avoid the public areas of the ship—I couldn't risk running into my fan club while holding hot stuff like this (I'm no prude, but I have a reputation to maintain). Once inside my cabin, I slammed the door behind me.

"Ernest? Is that you?" Celeste called to me from the other side of the connecting door. She must have heard the door shut.

I searched for a place to hide the photos. I shoved them under the bed mattress—no good, the maid would find it when she changed the sheets.

Celeste knocked on the adjoining door. "Ernest? Can I come in?"

"Wait a sec, I'm, ah, I'm changing clothes." I opened the closet door and shoved the envelope and the photos beneath my suitcase on the top shelf. Then I shut the closet door and wondered why I was I acting like an idiot, because Celeste couldn't see the pictures.

"You can come in now."

She entered the room. "Why are you panting?"

"Am I?" I took a deep breath to calm down. "I ran up the stairs to get some exercise."

"I thought you worked out in the gym."

"Well, you know, never hurts to get in a little extra."

"Don't wear yourself out before the show tonight."

The message light on my phone was blinking. I picked up the receiver, punched the button and listened to the recording before I hung up.

"Cinnamon left a message on the phone. She's waiting for me in the Leo Lounge. I have to go."

"Are you rehearsing?" she asked.

"Yeah, we're running through the dances."

"Can I go with you? I want to practice my songs."

"Why? You sounded great last night."

"I haven't done these songs as much as you have. I want to make sure I don't forget."

I couldn't refuse a request like that. She strapped on her fanny pack, slipped on her dark glasses, and picked up her cane. Once we reached the lounge, I was glad Celeste was with me, because we needed an accompanist for my dances. Celeste played the Yamaha while Cinnamon and I worked on the steps. Celeste got a little flustered, because she was used to playing the songs straight through, not the stop-and-start of only few bars at a time. But once she got the hang of what was needed, she was fine. When we finished dancing, Celeste kept playing the songs on her own, while Cinnamon and I sat at a table in the back of the lounge and changed out of our dance shoes into sneakers (me) and sandals (she).

"So, are you enjoying the cruise?" I asked.

"I was, until that woman turned up dead in your dressing room," Cinnamon replied.

"Really? What woman?"

"Oh, Sandy, don't play innocent. I think half of the

passengers know about it by now. Why didn't you tell me last night?"

"The security chief ordered me to keep quiet or I'd walk the plank. The victim's name is—was—Jodie Russ. She was a singer in the Starlight Ocean Revue. That's really all I know about her." That plus the fact she was cozying up to at least one well-heeled passenger.

"That must have been a terrible shock for you, finding her body like that, especially on the first night at sea."

"You haven't told anyone, have you?"

"Only Garvin. The news upset me, and I had to talk with someone. But he won't spread it around. He works as a jeweler, so he's discreet about other people's business."

"By the way, has he emerged from his lair? I've never seen the two of you together. I assumed you were on a romantic getaway."

"That's what I thought too." She sounded disappointed. "But once we got on board, Garvin spotted some business associates, and he went off to meet with them."

"Smart guy. Now he can deduct the cruise as a business expensive." Celeste was playing one of my ballads, perfect mood music for my next question. "If Garvin is tied up with schmoozing, I'd be happy to show you around the ship." If her beau wanted to waste a cruise with networking, maybe I'd have a chance to steal his girl.

She smiled. "That sounds delightful."

"How about lunch? All of that hoofing made me hungry."

"Terrific. How about the buffet by the pool?"

"No, too crowded. There's a little café on the Nocturnal Deck."

"Sounds cozy. Let's go."

As Cinnamon picked up her purse, I walked to the edge of the stage. "Hey, Sis." She stopped playing. "Cinnamon and I are leaving for lunch."

"Can I come along?" she said.

As much as I yearned for some alone time with Cinnamon, I'd look like a cad if I deserted Celeste. "All right." I met Cinnamon at the table. "My kid sister wants to tag along."

"Don't be grumpy. Celeste is a charming girl."

Celeste turned off the Yamaha and then we took the elevator up a level to the Nocturnal Deck, home of the Gemini Café and Bar. In honor of its name, the little restaurant had two molded plastic chairs on each side of the square tables. A pair of waitresses served each guest. At this time of day, the clientele consisted of mostly older adults in quiet conversation with their tablemates—the young families and kids were no doubt by the pool. To my irritation, though, every table was occupied.

"Looks like we'll have to eat in the dining room," Cinnamon said.

"If we do, I'll have to go and change clothes," I said. That would waste precious time, and Garvin might show up by then.

"Sandy, is that man waving at you?" Cinnamon asked.

Sure enough, the occupant by the back wall was signaling for us to join him. Aaron sat by himself at a table. No, not really alone—Moze was perched on his knee.

"Who is that?" Cinnamon asked. "Is that someone you know?"

"Yes, I'm afraid so." I said.

I wasn't keen on having lunch with this guy and his doll, but maybe the three of us could eat quickly and be on our way. So we sat, Celeste on my right (we used this seating pattern at the home dinner table so my left arm wouldn't bump her as I ate), Aaron—with Moze—directly across the table from me, and Cinnamon next to him. The ventriloquist was halfway through his shrimp salad. I could swear that Moze gave me the evil eye as I sat down—that's eye, singular, because one of the sockets in his face was empty.

The dummy turned his head toward Cinnamon. "Hubba hubba! This must be the tasty dish I ordered!"

Cinnamon, understandably, pulled back and stared at the doll. "What is that?"

I said, "Ladies, let me introduce Aaron Goldstein. He does a ventriloquist act on the ship. And that's Moze. This is Cinnamon Lovett, my choreographer, and Celeste Farmington, my sister."

"Hi, everyone," Aaron said. "Thanks for joining me. On these cruises it gets tedious to eat alone every day."

"Alone!" Moze exclaimed. "What am I, sawdust? I'm your best buddy. And why do you want to associate with these lowlifes anyway?"

"I beg your pardon!" Celeste said.

Aaron forced a smile. "Don't mind Moze. He's always joking."

"And Aaron boy isn't," the dummy replied. "Especially when he's on stage."

Celeste whispered in my good ear, "Why is that man so rude?"

"He's a dummy."

"I know that, but why—"

"He's a ventriloquist's dummy."

"You're kidding."

A set of identical twins, two waitresses in short skirts and sailor shirts and hats, stopped by to take our orders. The gals wanted hamburgers, fries, salads and soft drinks. I skipped the burger and fries for just a salad and unsweetened iced tea. I still hadn't worked up a taste for diet soda.

When the waitresses left, I said, "Aaron, can my sister take a look at Moze?"

He looked confused. "Sure, he's right here."

I hated having to explain my sister's disability. You'd think her sunglasses would have given the guy a hint. I nodded at Celeste, pointed to my eyes and then at hers, hoping the knucklehead would get a clue without me having to draw pictures. I guess he did, because his face lit up with a modicum of understanding. I took my sister's hand, reached across the table, and placed her fingers on the dummy.

She felt the wooden head and its natural hair. "It's missing an eyeball."

"Hey, watch it, toots," Moze said. "Don't go poking the other one out."

"What happened to the eye?"

"I don't know," Aaron said. "I didn't noticed it was gone until this morning. Maybe it fell out in the lounge after the show last night. Don't worry; I have spares in my cabin. I'll fix you up, Moze, when we're finished eating."

"I should hope so, or you'll have to introduce me tonight as the Cyclops."

Celeste said, "That's amazing. Why did you bring that thing in here?"

As I've said before, my hermit sister is a bit fuzzy on conversational skills.

But fortunately, Aaron didn't seem offended. "Moze goes everywhere with me. We're a team. That's why we work so well together."

Moze jumped in. "Oh yeah? What about the time you were shacking up with that Jodie creature? All I saw was the inside of a box. Can't tell me that witch was better company than me."

Aaron looked at Moze. "I had to spend time with her. She was my wife."

"But not for long!" Moze sounded ecstatic. "Her cutting out was the best thing that ever happened to us!"

"Moze, please."

Good thing the waitresses arrived at that moment. The food provided a distraction from the Aaron-and-Moze show. The ventriloquist returned to his salad (fortunately, Moze couldn't talk while his master ate), and we lit into our own dishes. First, I told Celeste how the food was arranged on her plate so she wouldn't have to paw around. She asked for the ketchup. A rack in the center of the table held plastic packets of condiments and paper napkins. I scooped up a handful of ketchup packets—she loved to soak her food—and placed them in her hand. Celeste set most of the packets beside her plate, tore one open, placed a hand on her fries and squirted the red stuff on the food. Out of habit, I grabbed some napkins and placed them in her hands so she could wipe her fingers. I glanced at the others. Aaron wasn't watching; Cinnamon just smiled.

After a few moments, I resumed the conversation. "So, Aaron, were you married to Jodie while the two of you worked on the ship?"

"That's right. Originally, Moze and I were part of the Starlight Ocean Revue. That's where Jodie and I met. For a while it was fun doing the show together but—well, you know. People change. After we split up, my contract with the revue was cancelled. I'm sure she had a hand in that. A few months later, the cruise line gave me my own show. Last night was my debut as a solo act. It was okay, but the audience was nothing compared to the crowds I played to in the showroom."

"We don't need those turkeys." Of course, Moze had an opinion on the matter. "We're better off without that hussy and her lame vaudeville act. That revue is so outdated, they're still using candles for the stage lights."

With Aaron literally talking out of both sides of his mouth, I had no idea how he really felt about anything.

I asked, "Did you love Jodie?"

"I was crazy about her," Aaron said.

"But she didn't give a tumble for you," said Moze.

Cinnamon cut in. "Celeste, how is your food? My burger's delicious."

"It's fine," Celeste replied.

Aaron continued undaunted. "When Jodie left me, I was so devastated, I couldn't work. This cruise is my first gig since the divorce. My comeback, so to speak."

"Really?" I said. "It is for me too. I haven't done a solo concert in years."

"Looks like we're both starting over. Clean out the past, a fresh start."

Moze sneered. "Yeah, with Jodie the jerk out of the way, it's full speed ahead, happy sailing!"

Aaron had finished his salad, so he excused himself, loaded the dummy into the black case, and left. The three of us breathed a collective sigh of relief.

Cinnamon watched him leave the café. "Interesting man, isn't he?"

I said, "I've never met anyone who could carry on a conversation with himself."

"I wonder if he knows Jodie is dead?" Celeste said.

"That's hard to say," I said. "If he loved her as much as he claimed, seems to me her death would hit him pretty hard."

Cinnamon, finished eating, wiped her mouth with a napkin. "What was it the dummy said right before they left? 'With Jodie out of the way, it's full speed ahead.'"

"He could be referring to the divorce," I said.

Celeste spoke softly, "Maybe Aaron killed her!"

"That sweet little man?" Cinnamon said.

"Don't let him fool you." I pushed my empty plate out of the way. "A guy who carries around a ventriloquist's dummy like a pet has a dark side I don't want to mess with."

We left the café. Celeste wanted to take a nap, and she

insisted she could find her way back to the cabin. I was glad she was finally feeling comfortable with moving around the ship on her own. I wasn't concerned about her getting lost. The elevator buttons had Braille markings; a recorded voice inside the cab announced the deck number when the door opened. The rooms had raised numbers on the doors. With cane in hand, Celeste set out. At long last, I could spend some quality time with Cinnamon.

Or not.

"There you are! Where have you been? I thought you'd fallen off the ship." A handsome young man confronted Cinnamon. He was my height, tanned and buffed with a mound of jet-black hair. His shirt was unbuttoned halfway down, showing a hairy chest.

I stepped up to him. "I beg your pardon!"

Cinnamon touched my arm. "It's okay, Sandy. This is Garvin Lee, my traveling companion. Garvin, Sandy Fairfax."

"Sandy." He gave my hand a quick but firm shake. "Cinnamon's told me a lot about you."

"I enjoy working with her. She's a great choreographer."

"Yes, she's quite talented. Now if you'll excuse us, I'm taking Cinnamon to lunch."

"I've already eaten," she said.

"You have?" Garvin was shocked.

"You were busy with your meetings, and I was hungry, so I ate with Sandy." He shot me glance. An edge crept into Cinnamon's voice. "I didn't know how long I was supposed to wait for you."

"My business went on longer than I expected," said Garvin. "Time slipped away from me. But that's all right now. I have you for the rest of the day."

"Cinnamon, will you be at the concert tonight?" I asked.

She turned to her friend. "Garvin, let's see Sandy tonight. You'll love his show."

"I'd rather see the comic. I hear he's terrific. What's his name? Aaron Goldstein, that's it."

She looked at me with panic in her eyes. Apparently she had no desire for a repeat of her luncheon encounter with Mr. Two-face.

"I have to help Sandy's sister with her makeup before their show," she said.

"That might be a problem," said Garvin. "If we don't head to the lounge right after dinner, we won't get the good seats. I hate sitting in the back and looking over heads."

I said, "Cinnamon, I'll have Celeste backstage by seven-thirty. That'll give you time to work with her and still make the other show." I said to Garvin, "Don't worry about seating. Most of the seats don't fill up until right before curtain time."

"That's good to know. Catch you later." Without another word, he took Cinnamon's hand and whisked her down the hallway.

So much for my plans of an afternoon of seduction. What did she see in that guy? He was pleasant enough, but something about his attitude grated on me. Anyway, speaking of seduction, the Libra Casino was right next door to the Gemini Café. The flashing lights and cha-ching of the slots was music to my ears. A couple of hours of gaming would nicely kill the time and take my mind off murderers and boyfriends.

When my teen idol career tanked in 1980, I spent much of my unemployment days with the high rollers in Las Vegas. After a few months of embarrassing myself with heavy losses, I learned the games, stayed sober while I played, and honed my skills until I started to win regularly.

Inside the casino area, I bypassed the Caribbean stud poker—I could get suckered into that game for weeks—but a chair opened at a blackjack table, and I slid in. The other players recognized me, but after some quick introductions we soon got down to the business of gaming. I soon hit a lucky streak and won consistently. A waitress in a black halter top and miniskirt stopped by to take my drink order, but I declined. After an hour or so, I'd built up a nice haul, so I quit while I was ahead and gathered my chips. On my way to the cashier, a familiar voice beckoned me.

"Sandy Fairfax! My good luck charm!"

"Hello, Tommy." How did these guys find me? I didn't need to see the almost-empty glass in the pianist's hand to know the waitress had served him a few too many drinks.

"So, how's Lady Luck treating you?" he said, his words slurring slightly.

"Just fine. I'm on my way to cash in my chips."

"Good for you." He draped his free arm around my shoulders. "And when you're done with that, I want you to have a drink with me so we can celebrate."

"What are we celebrating?"

"Today's a red letter day, my good man! Jodie Russ is dead!" He raised his glass. "Hallelujah! I'm a free man!"

Chapter 11: The Walls Have Ears

Tommy's remark intrigued me, so I agreed to a chat. First I deposited my chips with the cashier and asked to have the funds applied to my cruise expense tab. Then I ordered a daiquiri virgin from the casino bar while Tommy refreshed his gin cocktail. If the pianist was going to spill a confession on me, I wanted a quiet place to talk, so we took our drinks down the hall to the Virgo Library/Card Room. Just our luck, the room was empty, so I closed the door and we settled in the plush brown leather chairs amid the bookshelves filled with travel books and popular fiction.

"I take it you're not a fan of Jodie," I said, hoping to get his tongue wagging.

And wag it did. "That little scam artist? She had so many suckers caught on her hooks it was all bound to sink her someday. That gal had a singing voice, I'll grant you that. She could have lit up Broadway ten times over if she'd had the gumption. But she was too lazy to earn a buck the honest way. She stayed on this garbage scow so she could run her flim-flam games on the old rich guys. While their wives were off shopping or roasting to a crisp by the pool or getting pampered in the spa, Jodie moved in. By the time her poor mark found out he'd been fleeced, he was back home with his Botoxed wife, and Jodie was worlds away on another cruise."

"I take it you were one of her victims."

He drank and then laughed. I can't imagine why the police don't serve alcohol during interrogations—it seems to get people talking. "She had all kinds of angles going—

selling fake souvenirs, prostitution, blackmail—"

That explained the photos I'd found in her dressing room. Jodie must have been using them to bilk a hapless passenger she'd bedded down.

"—and loan shark. You might have noticed I like to wager. It gets pretty dull aboard the ship during the day. Once you've seen the tourist traps on Nassau, that's enough. So I gamble. Sometimes I don't play well. The casino is strictly cash and carry, no credit. That keeps the passengers from skipping out without paying up."

"Let me guess. You owed money to Jodie."

"You got that right, buddy. First loan was a freebie. Then she started upping the interest. When I complained, she threatened to report me. The big wigs running this pleasure jaunt don't like their employees in hock. They say it makes us sus—sus—"

"Susceptible," I said. The liquor was going straight to his brain.

"Yeah, that's it. Makes them 'sippable' to bribes. Half of my pay was going to that swindler. Last night she wanted me to pay off the whole bill. I get good tips for entertaining the rabble, but not that good."

"Did you see Jodie last night?"

"I was 'pose to. After dinner we both went straight to work: me to my piano, and she to the showroom. I was 'pose to meet her around nine-thirty."

"Aren't you playing at that time?"

"I do forty-minute sets and then take a break. In the revue, Jodie's finished with her yodeling by then. That's when I'd pay her. I'd go to her dressing room while the rest of the cast was onstage. That way nobody saw us."

Sounded like a perfect set up to me. Tommy could have murdered Jodie during that time and been back in the Pisces Bar in time to establish an alibi.

"She didn't show up last night?"

"Naw. I waited around, but she never popped up. Then I hadda get back to my keyboard. Didn't bother me. I wasn't going to chase her down. Guess she didn't want my money."

"Did you see anyone else backstage?"

"Nope." He jiggled the ice in his glass. "Will you look at that. Empty again. Time for a refill." Tommy got on his wobbly feet and placed a hand on my shoulder. "Sandy Fairfax, I want to thank you for being so understanding in this time of grief for Jodie Russ."

"My pleasure." Even though he didn't seem to be grieving over the deceased.

He fingered the sleeve of his drink-holding hand. "Huh. I lost a cufflink. Oh, poop. One of my favorites too."

"I'm sure it'll turn up." I stood up as well. "Thanks for your time, Tommy. I enjoyed our chat."

"Sandy Fairfax, you're an all right guy."

I placed my glass on the library table and left the room with Tommy. The pianist returned to the Libra for more drinks and games; I headed to my stateroom. Playing detective can wear a guy out. As drunk as Tommy was, his story might have been bunch of bull. Maybe he killed her. Maybe Jodie had already been murdered when he arrived for the rendezvous. Perhaps he made up the entire story in a drunken haze. My head hurt trying to figure it out.

In my room, I took a nap. When I awoke, Celeste was bored, so we played card games in my cabin. She had special decks with Braille dots in the corners of the cards to indicate suit and number. She's a pretty sharp player. As I dealt, I told her about Tommy. As always, she found the weak spot in my theory.

"If Tommy was the killer," she said, "what did he do with the body? He'd have to hide it somewhere close to the showroom. He couldn't take a corpse into the piano bar with him."

"If you've seen some of the piano bars I've been in, a dead body would look right in place alongside some of the customers. Do you have any jacks?"

"Are you going to tell Laytana about the pianist? Go fish!"

I pulled a card from the pile. "I'm not going to tell her anything. If she wants to find the killer, she'll have to do her own leg work."

"Maybe Tommy had an accomplice. Someone else moved the body. Any threes?"

I handed her my two threes and she spread out a winning hand on the table. I told you she was a whiz at this. "Great. Now I'm looking for *two* people. The killer and the hired muscle."

Suppertime rolled around, and we stopped playing so I could dress for the dining room. I tried to encourage Celeste to join me, but she didn't feel like making small talk with a new group of strangers. Eating two meals in public in one day was a huge step for her, and I didn't want her upset right before show time. She assured me she didn't mind eating alone—she'd turn on the TV for company. But she promised to go with me tomorrow night for the formal dinner, the once-a-cruise night when the passengers dressed up and ordered from a special menu.

When I arrived at the performers' private dining room, only Rex and Nessie were on hand. The king of the cowboys was decked out in an embroidered jacket and western shirt. The daughter wore pale green pants with a matching sleeveless duster and white shell.

"Hello, Madam Balorinsky," I said. "You're looking rather fetching tonight."

Rex grinned. "Ah! So you caught my daughter's alter-ego topside. She's a woman of many faces."

"Stop it, daddy." She playfully slapped him. "Hello, Sandy. I hope you had a pleasant day."

"It's been intriguing. Where are the rest of our tablemates?" Not that I was anxious to break bread with any of them.

"I don't keep tabs on our partners in crime. We better not wait on those slowpokes. I need to hit the trail and set up a new illusion for tonight. The others can just put on a feedbag when they arrive."

I agreed. I had an early call myself so Cinnamon could do my sister's makeup. The three of us sat and placed our orders with the waiter. After he left, I admired the king-size chunk of turquoise holding his bolo tie.

"That's quite a rock you got there, Rex."

"My tie clips are gifts from my dearly departed wife, may she rest in peace. So what have you been up to? Doesn't look to me like you've been tanning on the poop deck."

"I had lunch with Aaron. And Moze. So what's the story with him and his dummy?"

"He's a fine boy, he is. And don't let that dummy and his big mouth fool you. Aaron's a crackerjack comic. Big mistake, kicking him out of the revue."

"Father and I caught his act during a dress rehearsal in port," said Nessie. "He's quite good."

"Why does he carry that dummy around?" I asked. "I hate to say so, but that's a bit unusual."

"That's how he copes," said Nessie. "Jodie explained it to me. When Aaron was a boy, one of his uncles sexually abused him. He never got over the trauma. At the time when he was growing up, people didn't talk about things like that. For a long time, Aaron didn't speak. Then he saw Edgar Bergen on TV. He kept pointing at Charlie McCarthy. His parents got him a dummy, and that's when Aaron began talking again."

I'd have to admit, turning into a ventriloquist was no doubt more fun and profitable than psychotherapy. "So

Moze lets Aaron say the things he really wants to say."

"There you go, partner," said Rex. "Wouldn't life be a hoot if we all spoke our minds like that?

I smiled. "What did Jodie think of Moze?"

Nessie continued. "At first they were just like any other married couple, crazy about each other. With Jodie around, Aaron didn't need Moze off stage. Then they started drifting apart, and the old habit returned. Jodie blamed the dummy for their breakup, but I think that was a convenient excuse. She wanted to leave him long before that."

"Was Jodie having an affair?"

Rex acted indignant. "Son, what kind of a question is that?"

"Maybe one of Jodie's old flames killed her last night."

"You got a point there," said Rex. "Jodie was a mighty attractive filly. Onboard a ship like this, full of young stallions all liquored up and looking to kick up their spurs, it's possible she had a fling or two. But if she did, Jodie wasn't the kind to kiss and tell."

Just then, Tommy sauntered into the room, with a fresh flower in his jacket lapel and a smirk on his face. He seemed more ecstatic than when I'd left him earlier.

"Greetings, one and all," he said. "Sorry, I'm late, but I hit a winning streak on the wheel." He slapped me on the back. Next person who did that would find his hand missing. "Sandy, I knew you were my lucky charm!"

I raised an eyebrow at him. "Sit down and eat something so you'll be sober for your show tonight."

"Matter of fact, the nights don't seem as long when I'm a little soused." He took a chair beside me. "That's what I like about you, Sandy. Always looking after me."

The waiter entered the room and took Tommy's order. After he left, the conversation jumped back into full neurotic swing.

"And what are we all gabbing about tonight?" Tommy

asked.

Nessie said, "Sandy's trying to figure out who killed Jodie."

"Ah, and has our boy sleuth nailed a suspect yet?"

"No, and I'm not a sleuth," I said. "I just played one on TV."

"So far, Aaron is our leading candidate," Rex said.

"Oh, really?" Tommy rested his elbows on the table and linked his fingers together. "Seems to me, you're not so innocent yourself, Rex Stevenford."

"Now lookie here, you greenhorn. I'll admit that gal was a burr under my saddle at times, but if you're implying—"

"Cut the cowboy act, Rex. That went out with Gene Autry." Tommy said to me, "That Texas twang is as fake as a jackalope. The closest he ever got to Dallas was watching the show on CBS."

"I'll thank you to show some respect to my father!" Nessie shouted.

"Don't get your panties in a twist, my dear. I never fingered your fine daddy as a murderer. Just a phony."

"Now if that don't burn my britches!" Rex threw his napkin onto his plate. His chair scraped across the floor as he stood up. "Come on, Nessie. It's time we went to work."

"But, father, I haven't eaten—"

"We'll get the kitchen to package up your steak to go." Rex stood and nodded to me. "Excuse me." To Tommy he said, "There's no excuse for you."

After Rex stormed out of the room, Nessie sighed. "Please excuse my father. He's been under a strain lately. Some personal matters."

"Of course," I said pleasantly. "Have a good show tonight."

"Thank you." She stood and nodded at us. "Gentlemen."

Tommy and I rose to our feet and then sat back down after she left the room. The waiter brought our orders and then left with the Stevenfords' carryout.

The pianist placed his napkin on his lap, rubbed his hands together and laughed. "What a pair! They should give up that two-bit magic shtick and take their righteous indignation on the road."

"Is Rex really putting us on with his longhorn getup?"

"I should say so." We ate as Tommy talked. "When I was a kid, I spent my summers with relatives in Houston, so I know plenty about Texans. One day I struck up a conversation with Rex and discovered that what he didn't know about the Lone Star state would fill the ship's hull. Some time ago when I was between cruises, I stopped by a library and did some research. I searched the Dallas phone book; looked up old newspapers on microfiche; called up the various magicians' organizations. Couldn't find any trace of the guy or his magic act before 1988."

"That's only five years ago."

"Exactly! And that's the time he started working the Zodiac. Now this might be a cheesy ship, but it doesn't hire amateurs. They wouldn't bring aboard a performer who, as Rex would say, was 'fresh off the farm.' So what was he doing before 1988?"

"Maybe Rex isn't his real name."

"Possibly. But Sandy Fairfax isn't your real name either." He grinned. "We all have our little secrets, don't we?"

I gave the salt shaker a firm jolt over my meat. I didn't like what he was implying. "My stage name isn't exactly confidential. And if you want to know my secrets, just pick up any tabloid in the supermarket. Do you think Rex could be the killer?"

"I can't see it. He's too full of himself. If Rex did Jodie in, he'd brag about it and send out a press release."

The conversation was giving me a headache. "Aaron hasn't show up for dinner."

"That's not surprising. Some nights he settles for an intimate feast in his cabin, just him and his dummy." Off my look, he said, "I'm serious. One night I stopped by his room on some matter. When he opened the door, dinner was set out on a table, and Moze was propped up in a chair with a place setting in front of him." Tommy narrowed his eyes at me. "You seem awfully keen on pointing a finger at one of us."

"I didn't kill Jodie, if that's what you mean."

"So you say. So how did she turn up dead in *your* dressing room?"

I glanced at my watch. "Look at the time. Gotta run." Actually I wasn't late at all—I just needed an excuse to escape this loony bin. Celeste had the right idea of dining alone in her suite.

Chapter 12: Are You Lonesome Tonight?

Life backstage, as usual, was chaotic before the first show. Everyone passing by my quarantined dressing room stopped and stared at the door, as if Jodie might magically reappear. Earlier in the day, Jackson had managed to persuade Laytana to let him inside the room long enough to remove my stage clothes and makeup. Thank goodness. I would have died if I had to use my sister's cosmetics. But sharing the small dressing room with Celeste wasn't easy. I sat at the table in the swivel chair and put on my makeup while Cinnamon worked on Celeste, seated on the stool. Cinnamon was dressed for a night on the town in a dark red, knee-length dress with a small slit up one side. She managed to move in such a way that the slit didn't reveal much—much to my disappointment. Cinnamon entertained us by describing her recent tour of the Queen Mary liner, now permanently docked in Long Beach, and tales of the numerous ghosts that lived aboard that ship.

"So what you're saying is that Jodie's ghost will inhabit the Zodiac?" I was highly skeptical.

"I think she's already here. When I got here tonight, I'm positive I heard a thump inside the locked dressing room."

"Really?" My sister is quite gullible.

"She's pulling your leg, Sis."

"No," Cinnamon insisted. "I'm sure I heard something."

Cinnamon was still talking about ghosts when I left to check on things for the show. I don't normally chat with the band before shows, but the guys were still upset by the death, so I gave them a brief pep talk. A uniformed security guard was hanging around backstage, possibly to make sure someone else didn't get bumped off—where was he last night? He never spoke to anyone, just glared at the passers-by.

My biggest shock was when the show began. I got onstage and saw Helen sitting smack dead center, front row. During the show, I avoided looking at her, a challenge since she constantly yelled, laughed loudly, and called to me, even during the slower numbers.

During my costume change, I told the security guard about the disruptive woman in the front row who was creating a nuisance. To my delight, during the second half of the show the guard discreetly escorted Helen out of the room. To my disappointment, following the concert she reappeared at the autograph table.

"You kicked me out, didn't you?" She spoke loud enough for the others in line to hear.

"I don't know what you're talking about," I said.

"That was rude."

"I was rude? Whenever you learn to shut your mouth and act like a lady, you'll be welcome to stay. Now if you will kindly move along for the next person in line."

Helen stepped aside, but hovered near the table until the line had dissipated. I whispered to Celeste, seated beside me, "Helen's here. You go on backstage while I get rid of her."

For once, Celeste didn't argue with me. The room cleared of everyone except for Helen and me. I stood up, keeping the merchandise table between us.

"Helen, don't make me ban you from the lounge."

"Ernest, why are you so mean to me? Why can't we revive that spark we had?"

"Because that flame nearly burned me alive. Helen, the ship is full of eligible young men who just might be desperate enough to want you. Why don't you go to the singles mixer up on the Lido Deck? We'd both be happier if you did."

"But I want you, Ernest."

"So do my fans, but at least *they* know when to leave me alone."

"Can't we at least have a drink together?"

"I told you before, I don't drink. And I'm not starting up again for you." The cleaning crew trotted into the room, rattling their brooms and mops. "We have to go now. They clear out the lounge after every show."

"Are you going to let me back in for your next show?"

"Only if you behave yourself. Now if you'll excuse me, I have to get ready."

We parted and went our separate ways. During the second show, Helen turned up again in the same spot. This time she was quiet—too quiet. For the entire hour she glared at me, arms crossed, never smiling, applauding or laughing. I found this rather amusing and picked on her with such lines as, "There's a lady in the front row who isn't enjoying my songs. She must have lost her hearing aid. Or maybe she turned it off when the show started."

I paid for that afterwards. Helen made her way to the autograph table again. "I played nice during your show and you insulted me! Now who isn't behaving?"

"Lighten up, Helen. You know me better than that. You can't sit smack dab in front of me during a show and act like a rock and then not expect me to react."

"I'm telling everyone on this ship that you have a rotten show."

"Fine. You do that. Nobody listens to a drunk."

Helen couldn't follow me backstage, so as soon as I finished with the autograph line, I beat a quick retreat to the dressing room. I showered and dressed while Celeste stayed out front to chat with an older couple captivated by her songs. Except for Helen, I had a great time tonight. I especially had fun with my call-and-response number, which can go on forever once the audience is wound up. I sang the line, "Tell me true," and then held out the mic as the crowd yelled back, "I love you!" Despite the gloom of the murder, the shows cheered me up. Celeste and I had some good vibes going during our duet. Our impromptu banter before the song was getting longer and funnier. Tonight the audiences were bigger and more responsive. Connecting with appreciative fans is a thrill.

When I finished with the dressing room, I stepped outside while Celeste changed into a calf-length dark skirt with matching jacket, a white blouse and low heels. She was anxious to roam the ship. She'd taken a long nap earlier and was now wide awake and restless. As for my threads, I was back in my dinner outfit of a leisure suit and collarless shirt, suitable for the ship's evening entertainment. Celeste and I ate a late dinner at the midnight pasta buffet and then joined the band for drinks in the Gemini Bar. Celeste had her usual nighttime brandy and I, of course, stuck with O'Doul's. An all-guy band can get crude, and I'm sure my sister's sensibilities took a beating. I could tell, because she was silent and didn't join in the rude humor.

After a reasonable time, I made our excuses and I left with Celeste. I thought we'd go topside for some fresh air when I spotted Cinnamon and Garvin, him in a suit and tie, entering the Scorpio Disco. Hmmmm—maybe I could pry her away from lover boy for a dance or two.

"Sis, you want to go dancing?"

She knew what I meant by that. Celeste never danced in public because she was too self-conscious of how she looked, but she liked to sit and listen to the music and feel the pulse of the beat. We followed the pair into the disco. Loud and raucous, the disco wasn't the place to bring a date for an intimate *tête-à-tête*. The white walls carried the

Scorpio motif with large black stylized scorpions and black zigzags. A mirror ball rotated above the raised lighted dance floor filled with middle-aged adults. The DJ spun upbeat tunes of the '70s and '80s. I followed Cinnamon and Garvin through the tightly packed crowd and to a tiny and tall white square table near a wall.

As soon as they sat, I slid into one of the two remaining black stools. "Hi, mind if I join you?"

The expression on Garvin's face clearly stated, "No!" but Cinnamon said, "Hello, Sandy, Celeste. Please, be seated."

"Come on, Cinnamon, let's dance." Garvin took her hand and pulled her to her feet.

She shot me a weak smile. "We'll be right back." Cinnamon set her black clutch purse on the table and placed my sister's hand atop it. "Watch my purse, okay?"

The pair left for the dance floor. Talking was impossible over the noise, so Celeste and I enjoyed the music until Cinnamon returned to the table—alone.

"Where Garvin?" I shouted.

"He had to use the restroom," Cinnamon said.

"If you're still in the mood for dancing, can I oblige?"

She gave me such a fetching smile I nearly fainted. I told Celeste I was leaving and then I took Cinnamon's hand. I'd only seen Cinnamon on a dance floor in "teacher" mode, but now that she was free to move she was dazzling. Even in high heels she was light on her feet. She followed my lead with precision. After Blondie's "One Way or Another," the DJ switched to a slow number, "My Love" by Wings. Fine by me. I took my partner's right hand in my left, placed my right around her waist and held her close. We swayed with the music. She rested her head against my chest. My heart nearly jumped out of my ribs. My head swam—was it her perfume, the music or the thought I was finally close to the girl of my dreams?

"Hey! What do you think you're doing!"

Garvin grabbed my arm and yanked me away from Cinnamon. I placed my hand on his chest and shoved. Garvin clenched his fists.

"Boys! Boys! Stop it!" Cinnamon shrieked.

The other couples stepped back and stared. A security guy started moving toward us. I took a deep breath. As much as I wanted to punch out Garvin's lights, a public brawl would land me in the brig—if cruise ships had such things—or at least cancel the rest of my shows for the week.

"I was just keeping her warmed up for you," I said to my foe.

"Well, don't." He put his arm around Cinnamon's shoulders and roughly pulled her against him.

"Garvin!" She stepped away. "The music is giving me a headache. I'm going to bed."

She rushed back to the table to retrieve her purse. Garvin and I both followed.

"Cinny, I'm sorry," I said. "I didn't mean to cause trouble."

"It's all right, Sandy." She got up on tiptoe and whispered into my good ear. "Thanks for the dance. It was lovely."

She left the disco with Garvin in hot pursuit. I was just about to go to the bar to get drinks when someone tugged on my sleeve.

"Helen! What are you doing here?"

"I'm here to have a good time, just like you," she said. "We can now, you know, with that floozy gone."

"You mean Cinnamon? She happens to be my choreographer and a good friend."

"Now it's just us, isn't it? Dance with me, Ernest."

"Sorry, Helen, I tore up my dance card. Sis, let's get out of here."

I helped Celeste to her feet. We hurried back to our staterooms. I'd had my fill of partying aboard the Zodiac.

WEDNESDAY: Key West, Florida
Chapter 13: Beginner's Luck

I was awakened, not by a phone call, but a persistent knocking on the connecting door.

"Ernest? Are you awake?"

"No, Sis." I buried my face in the pillow.

"I'm hungry. I want to get some breakfast."

"How can you be hungry after all you ate at the buffet last night?"

"You promised to take me to see Key West." I gave a loud groan. "You should get up, Ernest. It's a beautiful day. I was out on the balcony and felt the sun on my face. Why are you still in bed?"

"'Cause it's a beautiful day for sleeping in!"

I was going to lose this argument, so I kicked off the covers and stumbled out of bed. I felt like skipping the gym this morning—just walking around this huge ship was exercise enough. I threw on a tee shirt, shorts and sturdy sandals. I lathered myself in sunscreen and grabbed my sunglasses, room key and wallet, since I planned on going ashore. Celeste gathered up her fanny pack, cane, dark glasses and a floppy hat. We headed topside to the breakfast buffet.

We had just finished eating a light repast when I spotted Cinnamon on the deck, gazing out over the railing. The Zodiac had docked in Key West. Passengers were already heading down the gangway and onto land. Cinnamon was alone—if I played my cards right, maybe I could kidnap her and take her ashore before her jealous boyfriend found out. I excused myself to Celeste and crossed the deck.

"Fancy meeting you here," I said, resting my arms on the railing.

"Good morning, Sandy."

"Have you been here long?"

"For a while. I saw them take the body ashore. I'm sure that's what it was. Some police officers came on the boat, and later they left carrying a coffin."

"That's a rotten way to start the day. Did you leave Garvin locked up in his cage?"

She looked at the shore. "He went ahead on his own. Said he was meeting some jewelers in town. Sometimes I wonder why he asked me on this cruise."

"I wonder what you see in the guy."

"You won't believe this, but when we met he was quite sweet. I know him from high school. He wasn't popular, and I felt sorry for him, so I was nice to him. Never grew into anything serious, but we kept in touch over the years. He seems different now. I don't know why he changed."

"If you ever need a shoulder to cry on, I'm always here."

"Thanks, Sandy."

"Excuse me!" Bunny approached me. "Sandy, I hate to interrupt 'cause I can see you're busy—"

"No, not at all, Bunny. I was just talking with my choreographer. What's on your mind?"

"Oh, hi, Cinnamon. You do such a good job with the dances. We love it when Sandy dances. Anyway, Sandy, the girls in the fan club were wondering, tomorrow night, could you and Celeste have dinner with us at our table in the dining room? If you've got other plans, that's okay."

"Right before a show I'm pretty busy. How about lunch?"

"Let's see, tomorrow we're all having lunch in Nassau. How does Friday look to you?"

"Yes, Friday would be fine."

"Fantastic! We'll meet you in the dining room for the first sitting at noon. The girls will love this. And one more thing. Some of the girls are going to miss your concerts tonight 'cause they want to see the other performers. I hope you're not upset. But we'll all be back Thursday night for sure!"

"That's fine. Have a good time at the other shows."

"Thanks, Sandy! I gotta run. We're meeting a member of the fan club who lives in Key West. 'Bye!" She dashed off to rejoin the cluster of women watching from a distance.

Cinnamon smiled. "You're lucky to have such devoted fans. They really love you."

"I've learned never take the public for granted. When my career tanked, I couldn't give away tickets to my shows."

"Don't be so hard on yourself. Forget all that and look ahead. The future is bright and sunny."

I noticed a certain woman walking in my direction. "My immediate future looks pretty dismal."

Laytana was making a beeline for me, and she didn't look happy. But I don't think that woman would be pleased even if she won the casino jackpot.

"Mr. Fairfax!" she called. I contemplated jumping overboard and swimming ashore. "I'm glad that I found you." I wasn't.

"What is it today?" I said. "Find another body?"

"If you were thinking of going ashore, you'll need to change your plans."

"What! I can't get off this claustrophobic ship and have some fun? Are you afraid I'll hijack a plane to Cuba?"

"The Key West authorities are here. They want to ask you some questions."

"I already told you everything that I know about Jodie's murder, which is nothing at all."

"They still need to speak to you. I hope we can take care of that here without the need of transporting you to the police station."

"I promised my sister that I'd show her around town. Do you want to explain to her why that's not going to happen?"

Cinnamon chimed in. "Sandy, I have an idea. I met some nice ladies at my dinner table, and we'll be leaving for the city in a few minutes. I'm sure they won't mind if Celeste joins us."

"Are you sure? You'll have to stick tight to her. Celeste freaks out in strange places if she's left alone."

"I don't mind. She's good company."

I said to Laytana, "Is that all right with you? Can I at least tell my sister?"

The flatfoot followed Cinnamon and me to the lounger where my sister sat. Celeste readily agreed to the change in plans—she'd have more fun doing woman stuff than tagging along with her big brother. I followed Laytana to the security office near the bridge where I spent an uncomfortable morning with the Key West cops (or was it the Keystone Cops?) in an endless round of grilling. I nearly bit my tongue off in an effort not to sound sarcastic or angry.

Then the cops and I walked to my former dressing room where I showed them precisely where I stood when I discovered the body. The cops measured distances, searched the room for evidence, and generally wasted my time. I thought about sharing my observations about the suspicious characters I'd met onboard, but that would only lead to another round of mind-numbing questions. Without proof, my theories were as useful as a hole in a lifeboat. So I kept my mouth shut.

When the cops finally let me go, I didn't have enough time go ashore; the ship was scheduled to set sail in a couple of hours. So I ended up in the Virgo Library for a meeting of what the ship's event calendar called the Friends of Bill W.—a euphemism for Alcoholics Anonymous. The people in the room were surprised to see me, since I hadn't yet gone public with my recent sobriety. I talked about my reform efforts, and the others shared their encouragement. We had a good meeting.

I'd eaten a filling breakfast and had snacks stored in the stateroom, so I skipped lunch and caught up on my shuteye. Celeste returned about three-thirty as the ship prepared to cast off for Nassau. I suggested that we both get massages. All the commotion of the week had left me tense; a good rubdown would help soothe me. During my touring days, I got hooked on massages to the point that my entourage included a masseuse (it's not what you think—my handlers made sure to hire an old, stocky-built German masseuse who kept me on the straight and narrow). I called the spa. Someone had just cancelled a massage appointment, so we hustled topside. During our rubdowns, Celeste gushed about her adventure on land, the stores and lunch at the nice restaurant. I zoned out and half-listened. Nothing bores me faster than shopping unless cars or guitars are somehow involved.

We returned to our rooms to prepare for the formal dinner, the reason why ships have tux and gown rental shops. Before we left L.A., my father had given me one of his old single-breasted tux that I had altered to fit. My father, the concert maestro, lived in tuxedoes. Mother had helped Celeste shop for a dress. I hadn't seen it yet—she wanted to keep it a surprise.

Cinnamon stopped by to do my sister's makeup for dinner. I could hear them giggling and talking like schoolgirls in the next room. I knocked on the adjoining door, and Cinnamon told me to go away until they had finished. What is it with women and getting dressed? Takes them a day to look presentable whereas men can cover their nakedness in minutes.

Time was growing short. I was ready to sound the alarm when Cinnamon finally let me into the room. Celeste looked like a dream. Her long blond hair was swirled and pinned atop her head; she sported a flower over one ear. Along with a blue, floor-length gown, she wore a matching long-sleeve crop jacket. Her silver-colored accessories consisted of a sash, sandals, a silver clutch purse in place of her fanny pack and, of course, tons of jewelry. She even sported a new pair of dark glasses set with rhinestones.

"Sis, you look fabulous."

"Glad you approve," said Cinnamon. "Now I must dash off and get ready. Garvin bought me a new necklace that I'm dying to show off."

He's buying her jewelry? That sounded serious. I returned to my room to put on my finishing touches: the cummerbund and bow tie—not a fake clip-on but the real thing. My father taught me how to tie a tie before I could lace my shoes. I put on my black jacket and off we went. Celeste left her cane behind because she said it looked stupid with her nice clothes.

We arrived at the Aries Dining Room about ten minutes after six o'clock. The mood was festive. The well-dressed guests sipped before-dinner drinks as they mingled. The ship's photographer had a grand time snapping pix of everyone. I described some of the nicer outfits to Celeste. My fan club dressed up, some in attractive pantsuits and others in cocktail dresses. Bunny had a floor-length black skirt and a long-sleeve white silk blouse. Even my band got in the act. No tuxedos—I didn't expect that—but suits and ties. Instead of heading for the private dining room, I hung by the main door to catch a glimpse of Cinnamon.

And what a glimpse. Her low-cut green gown clung to her body like shrink wrap on a record cover. But what really snagged my eye was the hardware that covered her breasts: an enormous emerald necklace comprised of a web of gold chains set with numerous cut stones. She needed an armed bodyguard to protect that loot. Of course, Garvin was with her, clad in a decent suit and looking miserable. If I had a woman like that on my arm, I'd be dancing on the ceiling.

I figured her pouty boyfriend wouldn't dare pitch a fit in front of a crowd, so I approached Cinnamon. "You're beautiful!"

"Thank you, Sandy."

"That necklace is incredible. Looks like it belongs in a museum."

"Can I see?" said Celeste.

While Cinnamon let my sister touch the rocks, I said to Garvin, "How much did that cost?"

He looked frightened. "I got it wholesale. Why do you ask?"

"I've never seen anything like it."

Our mutual admiration society didn't last long. An elderly couple, both decked in their finest, entered the dining room. The woman screamed, gathered up her long skirt, ran over to us, and pointed at Cinnamon's chest.

"My necklace! You're the one who stole my necklace!"

Cinnamon started at the intruder and clutched the jewelry. "My friend gave this to me!"

The woman was undaunted. "It looks exactly like my missing necklace!"

Garvin said, "Ma'am, I don't know who you are, but I assure you that necklace was never stolen."

An older gentleman with a head of white hair and a goatee joined us. He introduced himself and the woman as Herbert and Edith Hocksteter. He further stated that he could definitely identify the necklace as belonging to his wife. A few months ago, photographs had been taken of their family heirlooms and his wife's jewelry for insurance purposes.

The maître'd stepped up. "What seems to be the matter?"

Mrs. Hocksteter aimed an accusing finger at Cinnamon. "That's my necklace! It was stolen out of my cabin Monday night."

"Did you file a report with the security office?"

Herbert said, "Of course we did. Now you can catch the culprit red handed!"

Cinnamon, terrified, stared at her boyfriend. "Garvin? What is going on?"

"Don't worry, Cinnamon. They're mistaken." He said to the woman, "Ma'am, I'm a jeweler. I've sold dozens of these pieces. It's a popular style. Naturally, you were eventually bound to meet someone who also had one."

"This is not a coincidence," said Edith. "My necklace went missing, and now another one just like it turns up."

"Does your piece have real stones?"

"Of course. I'd never be seen in cheap cosmetic jewelry. That necklace is an anniversary present from my husband."

"That proves you're wrong. This necklace is paste."

Cinnamon glared at Garvin. "This is fake? You gave me a fake necklace?"

"My dear, that means nothing. Wealthy people wear replicates to prevent theft." Garvin turned to Edith. "That's something you might consider, ma'am."

"I don't believe it," said the matron. "Those stones look real to me."

"I'd be happy to let a certified gemologist examine the necklace. In fact, I insist."

The maitre'd said, "We have a jewelry shop on board, sir." A popular shopping destination because jewelry purchased during a cruise is duty-free. "The specialist can look at the necklace when the store opens in the morning."

"That's fine with me," said Garvin.

"In the meantime, we should place the necklace in a safe to avoid any further confusion. Would you come with me to the security office?"

"With pleasure." Garvin held out his hand. "Cinnamon, please."

With tears in her eyes, she unclasped the necklace and dropped it into Garvin's hand. "Keep it. I don't want it back." She hurried out of the dining room.

"What's going on?" Celeste asked me.

I wanted to follow Cinnamon, but with my sister in tow and all of the people milling around, I didn't have a chance. As we headed for the private dining room, I briefly explained the situation to Celeste. The usual gang was already presented, and I introduced Celeste to them. We all sat and the waiter took our orders. Despite the great dishes listed on the menu, the furor over Cinnamon's necklace had sucked the life out of the evening for me.

Our dining companions had witnessed the confrontation as well. "So our shipboard stealer has struck again," Rex said.

"This has happened before?" I asked.

"Indeed," said Tommy. "The Zodiac is a floating black hole. Bring your valuables on board and they vanish— poof!"

As usual, Moze, fixed with a new glass eyeball, offered his unwanted opinion. "Yeah, that's how the ship makes money. The passengers have to buy more jewelry, 'cause the stuff they had with them disappears!"

"Don't the passenger use the safes in their cabins?" I asked.

"Passengers are like a herd of cattle at round-up," said Rex. "You tell them what they're 'posed to do, and they do just the opposite. Folks on vacation don't want to think about getting robbed. They're here for fun. They get careless. They don't want to memorize the safe combination, so they just stick their goodies under the mattress. Or they forget to put things away and leave their loot laying about."

"How long have the thefts been going on?" I asked.

"Hard to say," Nessie replied. "It's sporadic. We get a plethora of reports and then a lull."

"And it's hard to say which claims are legitimate," said Tommy. "Some people misplace their jewelry and assume it's stolen when they can't find it. Or they report a burglary just to collect the insurance money. Jodie had one of those cons going."

"That's it!" Celeste said. "Mrs. Hocksteter said her necklace went missing on Monday night. Jodie must have caught the burglar in the act and that's why he killed her."

"Not likely," I said. "The Hocksteters are probably in a suite like ours. Those rooms are two decks below the Leo Lounge. Someone would have seen the killer move the body."

"He could have hidden the body in something, like a big suitcase." Celeste continued. "Why don't they look at who was onboard during the cruises when the thefts took place? The thief couldn't sneak onboard after the ship left port."

"We got us a regular Nancy Drew in our midst," said Rex. "She's got a smart head on her shoulders, and a pretty one too."

I checked my watch. "Hate to eat and run, but Celeste and I need to get going."

"Same here, partner." Rex kissed my sister's hand. "Pleasure meeting you, ma'am."

She blushed. "Why, thanks."

I said my goodbyes. Celeste and I headed for the Leo Lounge.

"They seem like nice enough people," she said.

"They were on their good behavior tonight. That

necklace fiasco gave them something to gab about besides tearing into each other. I can't figure out Garvin. Why would he give Cinnamon such a gaudy piece of jewelry?"

"Women like to have pretty things."

"I know, but didn't she realize the thing was fake? A guy like Garvin couldn't possibly afford boulders that size."

"Maybe she wanted to believe that he could."

We'd not only reached an impasse in our conversion but also our dressing rooms. Now that the cops were finished analyzing my dressing room, I could once more reclaim the space, although I disliked sharing it with the memory of a murder. I stepped into the room's tiny bathroom, soaped up a towel, and wiped down the swivel chair where I'd found the body. A silly precaution, but can you blame me? I left the towel on the floor and reached out to take a pair of leather pants off the clothes rack when I heard a noise behind me.

Before I could turn around, someone grabbed my ponytail and yanked my head back. The assailant threw a cord around my neck and pulled hard in an effort to strangle me.

Chapter 14: Hard-Headed Woman

I dropped the clothes hanger and grabbed for the rope, but it dug into my skin. I gasped for air. I twisted my head to one side to give myself more breathing room. I couldn't reach the hands of my attacker. I felt light-headed but I couldn't afford to pass out. A distant memory kicked in and told me what to do. I raked the heel of my hard-soled shoe down my assailant's shin and rammed my shoe into the top of their foot. The person screamed and the cord dropped. I coughed and spun around to face my foe.

It was Helen, wearing black sweatpants and sweatshirt.

I slammed her back against the wall, grabbed her wrists and pinned them to the wall.

"What are you doing!" (that's the G-rated version of what I said).

"Ernest, please, you're hurting me."

"Hurting you? You tried to kill me!"

"No, I wouldn't—"

Jackson ran into the room. "What's all the noise? The audience can hear you."

"Helen tried to murder me!"

"No, no, I just wanted to get your attention," she protested.

"By choking me?"

"I couldn't kill you, Ernest. I love you."

I said to Jackson, "Call security, now!"

By now we'd attracted a crowd in the small room—the band, Cinnamon, Frank and a crewmember who was cleaning the floors. Helen was bawling hysterically. I felt her weaken, and I was getting tired holding her, so I set her in the swivel chair. She was crying too hard to attack me again, but I stood by in case she tried to make a break for it.

"What happened?" Frank asked.

"The room was unlocked, so Helen sneaked in and hid in the closet. Then she tried to strangle me." I stared at her. "The same way you murdered Jodie."

"No! No! I didn't kill anyone!"

"Of course you did. You left her here as a warning that I'd be next if I didn't cozy up to you."

"Ernest, no! I didn't!"

A security officer arrived. I told him what had happened. I suggested he take Helen to Laytana in the security office, but the guy said he'd escort her to the clinic so she could get a sedative.

"She's faking!" I said. "I've seen her throw these fits when she doesn't get her way."

Helen tried to talk, but her blubbering made her incoherent. She grabbed a handful of tissues off my makeup table and blew her nose. The officer took her away.

Jackson asked, "Can you still do the show, Sandy?"

I rubbed my neck. It felt a little sore, but the scarf would hide any bruising. I sang a few bars. Fortunately for Helen, my vocal chords were undamaged; otherwise, I would have strangled her myself.

"Yeah, I'm good. That nutcase isn't stopping my show."

"How did you get away from her?"

"Would you believe, I used a move from my TV show. We had an episode where a bad guy tried to strangle Buddy Brave from behind. Buddy kicked him in the leg. I never thought that worked in real life."

I told the band to get ready. I went next door to tell Celeste what had happened. I didn't want her hearing a distorted second-hand account. She was happy I was alive, but she was shaken nonetheless.

"Ernest, that's awful. Maybe we should keep the dressing rooms locked."

"No, I'll just be more careful next time."

"Can you check my room? Make sure nobody's hiding in here?"

The miniscule room didn't afford many hiding places, but I inspected the bathroom, the closet, behind the clothes rack and even under the makeup counter. "All clear. Now let's go; we've got a show to do."

Back in my dressing room, I changed into my stage costume without further incident. As I was putting on my makeup, Jackson came in and announced we had nearly a full house. That fact cheered me up. Either the guests had seen all the other acts and had nowhere else to go, or word of mouth had sold the show. After my introduction, I rushed on stage to generous applause. I felt great. Nothing more would ruin my day.

Wrong again.

During the first number, I checked out the audience. In a front row table to my right sat an older couple, still in their formal dinner clothes, watching me intently. The man looked familiar. Where had I seen him? When I figured it out, I was so dazed I nearly stopped singing.

I was looking at the man in the photographs I'd found hidden in Jodie's dressing room.

I knew the song well enough that I clicked on autopilot and kept going while my mind went elsewhere. No mistaking that lean executive face with the chiseled features, the piercing brown eyes, the thinning grey hair. Some people say the way to relieve stage fright is to picture the audience in their underwear, but every time I glanced in the direction of this couple, I saw the naked image of him in the photographs—a picture I yearned to delete from my mental data banks. I turned my gaze elsewhere and soldiered on, occasionally glancing back to make sure the couple hadn't left.

The hour passed. After another rousing, audience-pleasing performance, Celeste and I took our bows and left the stage. "Sis, you go on to the autograph table. I have to meet some people.

"What? Who?"

"Tell you later. Gotta go."

I had to catch the man before he left the lounge. I wasn't about to chase him through the ship—not while wearing skin-tight black leather pants, a shiny glitter shirt and a scarf. I hurried onto the stage. Fortunately, the couple had waited for the back tables to clear out before going. They were only partway up the aisle to the lounge exit. I jumped off the stage and caught up with them.

"Hello, I'm Sandy Fairfax. Thanks for coming to the show." I extended my hand.

The man looked surprised at my effrontery, but shook my hand nonetheless. "I found it amusing."

The woman—who looked too old to be a mistress or trophy wife—said, "You liked it, Robert, and you know it." To me, she said, "That was delightful, young man. Not our type of music, but very entertaining. And that girl on the piano—what was her name?"

"You mean Celeste?"

"What a pretty name! Lovely girl, and such a talented singer. She'll go far, I'm sure."

I said, "Yes, well, I didn't catch your names?"

He said, "Robert Markson and my wife, Wilma."

"So nice to meet you both." Then I realized I had nothing more to say. With his wife standing here, I couldn't very well ask Robert if he'd fooled around with the ship's diva. "Have you seen the other shows? The Starlight Ocean Revue?"

"We caught that last night," said Wilma. "The revue has a new girl singer. She's nice, but not as good as the one they used to have."

My heart pounded. "You've seen the revue before?"

"Yes, we took this cruise last year. You know, dear, that dark-haired girl who could hit those high notes? Remember her?"

I watched his face for a reaction.

"No, I don't recall," said Robert. "We see so many shows and plays."

Liar! I caught a flicker in his eyes and a twinge at the corner of his mouth.

She grabbed his jacket lapel. "Darling, where's your pin?"

"What pin?" he said.

"Your silver pin. The one the company gave you for twenty-five years of service. You always wear it with this suit."

"It must have fallen off in the cabin."

Jackson was giving me the high sign to get my butt behind the autograph table. "Well, goodbye," I said, "Have a pleasant cruise."

"Yes, you too, young man," Wilma said.

Robert gave me a pleasant enough goodbye and they were off. I made my way to the line of waiting fans that eyed me impatiently. Did Robert know that I knew? But what did I know? I had no proof that Jodie was blackmailing him. The photographs hidden in the dressing room may have been souvenirs from their fling. Some couples used boudoir photos as a turn on. I also couldn't prove that the businessman had murdered Jodie. Wasn't Helen, the killer, in custody? Or did the lack-of-security officer simply let her go free to roam the ship and make another attempt on my life?

Why on earth did I let Marshall talk me into working this cruise? At the rate things were going, this just might be my swan song.

THURSDAY: Nassau, Bahamas
Chapter 15: Trouble

The Zodiac docked in Nassau, New Providence Island, a little before noon. This time nobody was stopping me from going ashore, no matter how many dead bodies turned up. I slipped on a shirt, khaki pants, socks, walking shoes and my sunglasses. The sky was a bit cloudy, but the temperature was nice and balmy, not too hot, with a gentle sea breeze wafting in. While Celeste was still eating her breakfast at the buffet, I made a quick stop at the security office. This time I was happy to see Laytana.

"Did you charge Helen Wheeler with murder?" I asked.

"We've released her."

"What!"

"We questioned Ms. Wheeler intensively. She didn't know Jodie Russ. She had no motive to kill her. One of the crewmembers saw Ms. Wheeler in her room Monday night when he took dinner to her. He said she didn't look well, so it's doubtful she left the room later to commit murder. We had no reason to hold her."

"So she's on the loose to come after me again."

"Not exactly. Her erratic behavior last night was not what we expect from our passengers. After some discussion, we decided we wouldn't bring assault charges against Ms. Wheeler if she terminated her cruise immediately. One of my officers is escorting her to the Nassau airport so she can return to the States."

That was good news and bad. I was free from another attack from Helen, but her release also eliminated one of my prime suspects. I wasn't convinced Helen was innocent of Jodie's death. Maybe she staged last night's attack as a way to get off the ship.

"Am I free to go ashore?"

"Certainly, Mr. Fairfax. Nobody's stopping you. We know you'll return unless you plan to swim back to the States. The airports have been alerted in case you attempt to purchase a ticket."

Apparently, I was still a suspect in Laytana's mind, but at least I wasn't a ship-bound prisoner. I best scoot off the ship before she changed her mind. At one of the poolside tables on the Lido Deck, I found Cinnamon eating a light breakfast of orange juice and a bowl of cold cereal with milk. I slid into an empty chair beside her. She wore a tank top and shorts. Forget looking at the ocean—Cinnamon offered a better view.

"Good morning, Cinny. Got any plans for today?"

"Hi, Sandy. I wanted to go ashore, but Garvin flaked out on me again. He's been in Nassau before, and he hates the gimmicky tourist traps."

Seemed strange for Garvin to book a cruise for a place he didn't want to visit, but I wasn't going to argue with my luck. "You're welcome to go join Celeste and me. We're leaving right away."

"Thanks, that's sweet of you. Just let me finish eating."

"Take your time. What's the latest on the necklace mix-up?"

"The jeweler on the ship says it's made of glass. Garvin said he'll make it up to me and buy me a necklace with real gems, but it wouldn't be the same."

"Are you still going to wear the fake one?"

"I told him to keep it. What would I do with it anyway? Where would I wear a thing like that? I don't go to red carpet events or Hollywood parties."

"That's a shame. I thought you looked good in it. Made

your eyes sparkle."

She looked up at me and smiled. I nearly melted into the ocean. She finished eating; I collected my sister (she finally dressed casual today with a blouse and jeans), and the three of us disembarked. After being cooped up on the ship for three days, I felt great, stretching my legs and walking on a surface that didn't move. A number of other cruise ships were docked as well, spewing their ready-to-rumble passengers. Since all the ships stopped here, the area by Prince George Wharf was stuffed with tiny huts full of overpriced and often tacky merchandise, ready to snare the cash-landed saps as soon as they set foot on dry land. Garvin was right about the tourist traps.

We found some shops with higher-end items and I bought gifts for my two kids back home—and nothing for their mother, my ex. The merchants expected customers to barter, so with my natural gift of gab I landed some bargains. The three of us lunched on fried snapper at one of the native shacks. I was interested in renting a car and cruising around, but the gals, who wanted shop, outvoted me. At one open-air shop, Cinnamon and Celeste were busy rummaging through some racks of clothing the way that women do when they shop, so I amused myself by watching the pedestrians, especially a man who looked exactly like Garvin.

Garvin? What was he doing here?

He carried an attaché case, not the sort of thing a sightseer would lug around. I told Cinnamon I wanted to check out something on my own and then I handed over my packages to her so I wouldn't lose them. She seemed irritated at my request, but I set off before she could argue. I followed Garvin, staying far enough back that he wouldn't see me. He left the touristy area and headed into the city itself, a pleasant-looking town of wide lawns and neat one-to-two-story buildings. Foot traffic was sparse, so

I had no trouble keeping him in view. He entered a jewelry store set in a real building, not one of the tourist booths. The entire front wall of the shop was glass so I could see him. Likewise, he might also spot me, so I stood against the wall and peeked in occasionally to see what he was doing.

Garvin set the attaché case on the counter and opened it. He removed Cinnamon's emerald necklace from the valise and handed it to the jeweler. Was he getting a second appraisal—or trying to sell the piece? If Garvin were trying to pull a scam, the jeweler would immediately spot a fake. The employee make a careful examination of the necklace, set the piece in a box—and handed Garvin a huge stack of bills.

The guy must have two necklaces: one fake and one real. Maybe this second piece really was the stolen necklace.

Garvin placed the money into the attaché case, closed it, and left the store. I stayed with him. Just then, a family behind me shouted at their kids to settle down. At the sound, my prey turned his head. Before I could duck out of the way, our eyes met. Garvin shot off and ran from the dock. I kept up, just barely. He turned down Elizabeth Avenue and sprinted up the sixty-five stone steps of the Queen's Staircase. Who needs a gym when I can get a workout while playing sleuth?

At the top of the heart-attack hill, I stopped to catch my breath. Garvin ducked into the 126-foot-tall Water Tower, an imposing stone structure once used as a lookout for thieves (before our trip, Celeste had boned up on the city's history). How appropriate, since I was tailing a thief. I entered the tower and rode the elevator to the top. Garvin was the only person on the balcony except for the clerk minding a small merchandise table; those souvenir sellers were literally *everywhere*.

On seeing me, Garvin pulled some bills from his wallet

and slapped the money on the table in front of the clerk. "Take a break for ten minutes."

"Thank you, sir!" The woman left via the elevator.

Garvin turned his attention to me. "Why are you following me?"

"I was going to ask why you were in town. Cinnamon told me you were staying on the ship."

"She's got a big mouth."

"She also said the emerald necklace was a fake. Apparently, the local jewelers can't tell the difference between real and paste."

"What is that to you?"

"So why did you give Cinnamon a fake necklace and not the real thing?"

"Like I said last night, I wanted to keep her safe. I'd heard about the burglaries on the ship. I was going to give her the real necklace when we got back home. She said she didn't want it, so there was no point in keeping it. It fetched a better price here than what I could get in the states."

"Did you steal the real one?"

"I don't need to say anything to you. You're not a cop."

He had me there, but I'd played enough poker that I could still bluff. "If the security officers searched your cabin, would they find other stolen jewelry? Or did you sell that already? Is that what you've been doing at your so-called jewelers' meetings?"

"I didn't steal anything, and if you say I did, I'll deny it."

"If you're innocent, why didn't you tell Cinnamon about the real necklace?"

Garvin dropped the attaché case and pushed me hard in the chest with both hands. I stumbled back against the balcony edge. He stepped up and grabbed my shirtfront, pining me in place. I clutched his wrists, more to keep my precarious balance than to break free. If I struggled too much, I might go sailing backward over the ledge.

"Take it back!" he screamed.

I tried to stay calm. Yelling might upset him more. "Garvin, stop acting childish."

"Say you're sorry for calling me a thief!"

The rough stonework in the ledge pressed against the back of my legs. "Let me go, Garvin."

"Say you're sorry!"

I heard the clanking of the elevator cab and a stampede of feet on the floor. Garvin turned his head. The merchandise clerk and a cluster of middle-age Japanese tourists, all laden with cameras on neck straps, ambled out of the elevator. They gazed quizzically at us—or rather, me.

Then one of the women shouted, "Buddy Brave!"

The sightseers broke out in huge grins and nodded. "Ah, yes, Buddy Brave!"

The Japanese people loved American teen idols, and I was no exception. In the 1970s, my show was a huge hit in the overseas markets. I performed a couple of successful tours on that lovely island. Now that the visitors had recognized me, my sleuthing was finished. Garvin let me go and stepped away. The sightseers clustered around me. In the mêlée, the jeweler grabbed his attaché case and bolted for the elevator. The crowd was pressing in so much I couldn't run. I could never be rude to fans, so I put on my smile for them and posed for pictures.

By the time the photo session was over, Garvin was, of course, long gone. I left my fans on the balcony and returned to the ground floor. I figured Garvin would eventually end up on the ship. If he hid in the city or took a plane off the island, he'd look guilty. And there was no point in reporting the incident to the local cops. Garvin would deny that he tried to push me off the balcony, and I had no proof he was selling stolen merchandise. I checked my watch and realized I'd better get a move on it before the ship set sail. Maybe that was Garvin's plan—delay me on the island long enough to leave me stranded. I hailed a taxi for a ride to the wharf. The driver gouged me on the fare, but the trip was fast and I was onboard in no time.

On the Lido Deck's pool side Aquarius Stage, a dreadful guitar-and-drums band was murdering Top 40 hits during a best hairy chest contest among the passengers. A huge crowd was clustered around the never-ending buffet, looking for a light snack to hold them until dinnertime. Before I got far, the ship's entertainment director intercepted me. She asked if I'd seen Hugh and Mindy. She had to shout so I could hear her over the raucous band. She couldn't find them anywhere on the ship. I don't know why she thought I would keep track of those two, but I told her no; I hadn't seen them either on the ship or in Nassau.

As soon as she departed, I went on my way toward the elevator. I wanted to avoid the best hairy chest contest—no doubt the event organizers would love to rope in a celebrity contestant. I'd shown my bare chest enough times during my teen idol days, thank you. A straight line across the center of the deck—and through the thick of the crowd—would be the shortest route to my destination, but I wasn't in the mood to be cheery to strangers, so I took a longer but more restful path—the jogging/walking track around the deck.

I was alone on the track. The serious athletes had already jogged in the cool of the morning, and the casual walkers were out strolling on the island. To my left was the railing overlooking the harbor waters. To my right were the walls that formed the backside of the buffet restaurant and the pool house. Unfortunately, even at this distance from the pool I could still hear the awful band. Still, I relished the solitude. I enjoyed the distant view of the island, the seagulls overhead and the beauty of the waters below without having to look out for Celeste or think about a murderer.

The track made a curve. As I cleared the curve, two people jumped out from a narrow passageway between the buildings. Both wore long-sleeved black tee shirts and black pants. Ski masks covered their heads. With one on either side of me and without a word, they pushed me onto the deck. I yelled for help, but with the band pumping up the volume, nobody heard me. One of the attackers sat on my chest and tied a rope around my wrists. With that weight on me, I could barely breathe, and I couldn't roll away. I kicked, but the other assailant sat on my legs and deftly wrapped a rope around my ankles. I managed to raise my head enough to see that the rope fastened around my legs also passed through the hole of a large iron washer.

The attackers stood; one picked me up by the shoulders and the other by my ankles. They threw me over the railing into the deep harbor waters.

Chapter 16: I Don't Want to Be Tied

The two women entered Celeste's stateroom. "Where should I put your brother's packages?" Cinnamon asked.

Celeste dropped her island purchases atop the bed. "In his room. It's right next door." She knocked on the adjoining door. "Ernest? Are you in there?" She opened the adjoining door. "Ernest? Are you sleeping?"

Cinnamon peeked into the other suite. "He isn't in here."

"He isn't? That's strange. He always comes here before dinner to change clothes. Did you see him when we came onboard?"

"No, I didn't. Maybe he's still on the island." Cinnamon entered Sandy's room and dropped two armloads of bags onto the table. "The nerve of that guy. He asks me to hold onto his things and then he takes off and never returns. What was he doing, chasing after a girl? Celeste, I'm leaving his packages on the table in his room."

"Thanks. You're very helpful."

"The way your brother takes off for no reason, it's a good thing I'm here for you."

Cinnamon returned into Celeste's suite and closed the adjoining door behind her.

Celeste picked up the phone and called Jackson. "Have you seen my brother this afternoon? I thought he might be with you. No? Okay, fine. If you see him, tell him to call my room right away."

After she hung up, Celeste sat on the edge of the bed. "I'm worried. Maybe someone on the island recognized Ernest. He used to get death threats all the time. Maybe he was mugged or kidnapped."

"I don't think so. Most likely he just lost track of time. He gets a little absent-minded at times. Celeste, I'm going to look around the ship. Maybe he's in the casino or having coffee with someone."

"Would you? Thanks heaps."

"Don't mention it. I'm sure wherever your brother is, he's doing just fine."

* * * * *

I'd been tossed off a cruise ship before—on my TV show—but this time, no safety crew was standing by to bail me out. I struggled to stay calm—if I panicked I'd never get out of this mess alive. The surface of the water approached at top speed. I barely had time to tuck in my head, hold up my arms for protection (thankfully the villains didn't tie my hands behind my back), and sucked in a lungful of air before I smacked into the water. The force momentarily stunned me.

The tropical sun hadn't warmed up the water and my muscles cramped. With the iron washer tied to my legs I, well, sank like a stone. I pulled on my wrist ropes but to no avail. Something brushed against my head. I opened my eyes and the water stung them. Some fish swam by. Right now, survival was more critical than sightseeing. I landed on the harbor floor. If I didn't get rid of that iron weight, I'd never swim away. I bent over and tugged on the rope holding the washer, but the knot held firm. A stream of bubbles escaped from my mouth. My heartbeat was bypassing the speed limit. My anxiety was eating up precious oxygen. To make matters worse, the sharp points of the coral bed poked into my skin.

Sharp points.

I felt along the floor bed until I found a long, thick piece of coral. I snapped it off and used the broken edge to saw on my leg ropes. I felt woozy, but forced myself to stay alert. The rough coral cut into the skin on my palms. Frantic, I dug the impromptu saw into the bindings while fighting the urge to take a breath. Blood dripped from my sore palms. The blood coagulated and floated in the water around my head. I pushed a fish out of my face. Water seeped into my mouth; it tasted terrible. The rope fibers began to separate. I grabbed the frayed rope and yanked it apart.

With my legs freed, I looked upward and kicked like the devil. Between swimming laps in my home pool and dancing, I'd build up a strong set of legs. I paddled as best I could with my tied hands. My lightweight summer clothes soaked up water and felt heavy, slowing me down. My air was nearly gone. I kept my eyes focused on the surface. *Keep going. Keep going.* My legs hurt. My lungs were about to explode. One more strong kick—

My head broke free of the water. I threw my head back and gulped in the clean, fresh air. I closed my eyes and treaded water while I caught my breath and tried to think.

How was I going to get back on the ship?

* * * * *

The hairy chest contest had selected a winner and the band had, to everyone's relief, stopped playing just as Cinnamon stepped onto on the Lido Deck. She'd peeked into every bar, café and lounge on the ship, but had found no sign of Sandy. She'd questioned crewmembers, but nobody had seen him since he left the ship that morning. Maybe Sandy was in the cabin of a lovely young woman? And why did that thought make her intensely jealous? Exasperated, she started toward the stairs that led to the gym and spa. Maybe he was sneaking in a quick massage.

She spotted a familiar face a few yards away. "Madam Balorinsky!"

The lady interrupted her reading of a dowager's palm. "Yes? Who calls?"

Cinnamon ran to her. "Madam Balorinsky, have you seen Sandy Fairfax? Within the last hour or so?"

"Sandy Fairfax. Let me think . . ." She raked a long, red fingernail across her cheek. "Tall man, sandy hair, sexy and cute as a bug in a rug?"

"Yes, that's him. Have you seen him?"

"No, not today. Such a distinctive man. I would have remembered."

"Can you use your psychic powers to find him?"

"Alas, I cannot give a reading unless I actually see or touch a person. My regrets."

"Thanks anyway."

Madam/Nessie returned her attention to the dowager. "Ah ha! Your romance line breaks off but returns even stronger than before."

Cinnamon shaded her eyes and scanned the people on the deck. She questioned several persons until a crewman stated that he'd seen Sandy a short while ago, heading toward the port (left) side of the ship. But when Cinnamon walked in that direction, all she found was the empty jogging track. That didn't make sense. After all the walking they did on the island today, why would Sandy want to use the track? And why was she so concerned about him anyway? He wasn't her responsibility. Sandy was a grown man—he could take care of himself.

Cinnamon strolled along the track anyway, mainly to give herself time to think. First, her problems with Garvin and now, Sandy. Men were such a bother. She should just focus on her career and forget about romantic entanglements that were too hard to unravel. From now on, her relationship with men—especially Sandy—would be strictly professional. Singleness had its virtues—less drama, more control. Cinnamon turned and started back toward the pool area.

Something on the ground caught her eye.

She bent over to pick up two objects that were shoved against the wall—a keycard and a wallet. The items must have dropped out of the pocket of one of the joggers. She'd take the keycard and wallet to the lost-and-found at the information desk and, hopefully, the rightful owner would reclaim them. She flipped open the wallet. Normally, Cinnamon would never peek inside a stranger's personal belongings, but today she had a feeling that she should look.

Inside the wallet was a California driver's license issued to Ernest Farmington.

A chill ran over her. Sandy might be forgetful about some things, but he seemed the kind of man who would never lose his wallet. She glanced around.

"Sandy! Sandy! Where are you?"

Something moved in the water. Cinnamon leaned over the railing. "Sandy! Is that you?"

She clutched the railing and stared in horror. Yes, a man was definitely struggling in the water. Stunned, Cinnamon considered jumping in, but what could she do? She couldn't possibly tow a large man to shore. She glanced around for help. A white life preserver emblazed with "SS Zodiac" hung on the wall. The device appeared more ornamental than practical, but Cinnamon yanked it off the hook and threw it into the water.

She cupped her hands around her mouth. "Sandy! Grab the life preserver!" She strained her voice to be heard. "Hold on! I'm getting help!"

Celeste ran back to the pool. "Man overboard!" The passengers gathered at the buffet counter laughed, thinking this might be another entertainment stunt. She grabbed the arm of a waiter; he dropped his tray of drinks. The plastic glasses rolled along the deck, spilling their contents.

"Sandy's in the water!" she yelled. "Help him!"

The waiter pulled his arm away. "Miss?"

"There's a man overboard! In the water! I'm not kidding!"

"Ma'am, swimming is not allowed in the harbor."

"He fell off the ship!"

The floor shuttered as the Zodiac's engines hummed to life.

The waiter said, "The ship's preparing to sail."

"No! No!" She gripped his arms. "You can't leave! Sandy's in the water! You must save him!"

A man seated at one of the tables called, "Where's my drink?"

At the sound of Cinnamon's screams, other crewmembers gathered around. At last, someone believed her. Cinnamon ran back to the jogging track with the crewmen following. As soon as the crewmen saw the figure in the water, they sprang into action. The one who had a radio attached to his uniform called the engine room to order a full stop. The others began to lower a lifeboat. Cinnamon watched and sent up a silent, heartfelt prayer for Sandy's safety.

*****

I don't remember much about the actual rescue. I was too emotionally and physically spent. Someone on the ship bonked me on my noggin with a life preserver and almost knocked me out. But the thing floated, so I draped my arms over it and hung on. By now my legs were failing. I was barely treading water with my toes. Before the lifeboat arrived, I managed to work the ropes off my wrists. Some men pulled me onto the boat. Someone draped a blanket around my shoulders. I was soaked and shivering. I think someone talked to me, but I was too exhausted to listen— and water was still sloshing around in my ears.

What I remember most was stepping out of the lifeboat and seeing the look of relief on Cinnamon's face. She ran up and hugged me. She didn't seem to mind getting wet from my dripping clothes. I tried to say something to her, but instead I passed out in her arms.

Chapter 17: Doin' The Best I Can

I woke up in a narrow bed with a rock-hard mattress and stiff white sheets. A fluorescent tube flickered in the ceiling overhead. The room stunk of disinfectant. The palms of my hands were wrapped in bandages. My long hair hung loose over the pillow. I felt sore all over, no thanks to the various bumps and bruises. I was wearing a white open-back hospital gown—what happened to my clothes?

Cinnamon sat in a straight-back metal chair beside the bed, knitting. A bag full of yarn rested on her lap. She'd changed into a nice blouse and slacks outfit. She was so focused on her work, she apparently didn't notice me waking up.

"I didn't know you could knit," I said.

She looked up from her needles. "I do it to pass the time when I'm traveling or waiting off stage during a video shoot. How do you feel?"

"Like the ship's anchor dropped on my head." I rubbed my eyes and blinked. "I take it I'm in the ship's hospital?"

"After you fainted, the crew carried you here on a stretcher."

"How long have I been here? Where's Celeste? She must be worried sick about me."

"Celeste was here for a while. She was getting antsy, so I told her to wait in her cabin and I'd call when you woke up. How did you manage to fall off the ship?"

"I didn't fall. Two goons tied me up and threw me overboard."

She frowned. "Really, Sandy."

"I'm dead serious, and I do mean *dead*."

"Why would anyone want to do that to you?"

"Because I'm uncovering everyone's dirty little secrets."
I started to tell her about my towering encounter with
Garvin when a thought crossed my mind. "What time is
it?"

She glanced at her watch. "Almost eight o'clock."

I sat up in the bed. "Eight o'clock! I have to get ready
for the show! Where are my clothes?"

"I sent your wet clothes to the cleaners. They'll be
delivered to your cabin."

"You're awfully good to me."

She sighed. "Someone has to look out for you."

A nurse in a starched white uniform, and an equally
rigid expression, entered. "Mr. Farmington, I'm glad to see
you're awake. I need to take your vitals and then you can
get some more rest."

"I'm rested. I have a show to do."

"Mr. Farmington, you are in no condition to perform."

"Look, missy, I've never missed a show in my life, and
I'm not starting now."

The Florence Nightingale pretender turned to Cinnamon.
"Please tell your husband to calm down."

Cinnamon smiled. "I'm afraid that isn't possible. He can
be pretty stubborn at times. And he isn't my husband."

"She's my choreographer," I explained.

The nurse shot me a dirty look. "Your what?"

Obviously, this uneducated woman was confusing
"choreographer" with a different profession. And I was
entrusting my life to this idiot?

"Dance teacher," I explained.

Dr. Carpenter entered the room. "How's our patient
doing?"

I pushed back the covers and swung my legs over the
edge of the bed. "Hi, doc, you're just the man I need to see.

The patient is doing just fine, and he has to get on stage as soon as possible."

"Oh, no, you don't. Get back in that bed."

"Doc, I feel fine, honest. I have a concert in a few minutes. People are depending on me."

"You won't be doing them any good by leaving before you're ready."

"I'm ready." I got on my feet and started for the door. Then my knees buckled and my head swam. I reached out to hold the table for support and missed.

The doctor grabbed me and stopped my fall. "No, you're not." He helped me back into bed.

"Can't you give me something to, you know, get me back on my feet? Something to keep me going for the next couple of hours?"

"Mr. Farmington, most people would relish the opportunity to relax and not go to work."

"Look, doc, I'll make a deal with you. At least let me do the second show tonight. Then it's straight back to bed, no late night parties. It's my last night of concerts on the ship, and I can't miss that."

"I have a feeling if I say no, you're going to sneak out anyway. All right, Mr. Farmington. If you get some more rest over the next two hours, and your vitals are good, and you can walk without falling, I'll see about releasing you. But no promises."

"Thanks, doc. And, Cinny, can you get me some clothes? I'm not walking through the ship dressed like this."

She grinned. "I don't think I will. That gown looks good on you."

For a moment, I thought she was serious.

* * * * *

Cinnamon woke me at nine-thirty. I still felt weak, but I was determined to get back on stage if only to thumb my nose at the creeps who dunked me earlier. I was starved, so the nurse brought me a dinner tray with bland roasted chicken, canned fruit and canned veggies heated up. Seriously? The dining room was serving lobster tonight, and this was the best the kitchen could scrounge up? Nurse Ratchet claimed this was the standard "sick call menu." Good incentive to stay healthy. But despite the taste of the food, I gobbled it up—if I had an appetite, maybe the doctor would release me.

Cinnamon, bless her soul, brought me a clean shirt, pants, underwear, socks and shoes. After I dressed, she walked with me to the Leo Lounge with orders from the doctor to rat me out if I collapsed. To save my strength for the stage, I went straight to my dressing room and didn't see anyone. I took a shower to get rid of the grit and smell of the seawater.

When the ten-thirty show started, I was thrilled to see a packed house. The people who had planned to see the first show were here along with the late diners; extra chairs had been added in the aisles to accommodate the overflow crowd. I lacked my usual vigor, but the audience was so enthusiastic I tapped into their energy and pushed on. With my hands still bandaged, I skipped my acoustic guitar solo and substituted one of my B-side ballads, "The Picture in the Locket." Despite the change, the audience members were generous in their affection. Either they knew about my soaking and felt sorry for me, or else being near the end of the cruise they were too tired to critique. Since this was my last show of the week, my fan club was extra vocal. Their affection perked me up. But I still felt a nagging sense of foreboding.

As I sang the opening numbers, I scrutinized the audience. Were my attackers here? Did they come to see if I'd escaped their death trap? I saw a number of unfamiliar faces in the crowd—or had I met two of them earlier on the jogging track?

The band played softly behind me as I greeted the guests. "Hi, welcome to the show. We're glad you're here. I'm glad I'm here. On behalf of the band and our special guest, Celeste Farmington—" I turned to face my sister. I hadn't seen her since I'd left her shopping in the market. I stared at her and motioned for the band to stop playing.

"Sis, what on earth did you do to your hair?"

Celeste sported a headful of long, thin braids, each strand tipped with colorful beads. She shook her head and the braids swung about, the beads clinking together. "Do you like it?"

"Looks like you got your hair caught in an eggbeater."

"The native women on the island did it. They have a hair braiding business right on the wharf."

I turned to the audience. "This is what happens when I leave my sister alone for five minutes."

"You're jealous, Sandy," she said. "I bet you'd look cute in braids. Anybody else think Sandy would look good in braids?"

My fan club roared its approval. A word of warning, guys—never do a live show with your sister, especially not after she gets comfortable with improvising.

I gave the audience a woe-begone look. "Ladies and gentlemen, my sister, the sit-down comedian."

After the applause died down, we got back on track with the show. But I got in the last word. When I sat on the bench for our duet, I pushed the braids out of her face. "Sis, are you in there somewhere?"

All things considered, the show went well and ended with a standing ovation from the entire audience. I wished Celeste could have seen it, but at least she heard the clapping and cheers. At the autograph table, Bunny reminded me of my luncheon appointment with the fans tomorrow. I'm glad she told me; with all the craziness that had happened today, I'd forgotten.

With the large crowd, signing autographs took longer than usual. By the time I finished, I was drained. I retired to my dressing room, sat in front of the makeup table and wiped the junk off my face with a tissue. If I took a shower, I'd fall right to sleep. Celeste knocked on my open door. I directed her to the empty chair beside me.

"Cinnamon told me what happened to you," she said. "I'm sorry I wasn't with you in the hospital."

"Don't worry about it. There's nothing exciting about watching me sleep."

"She said two men threw you overboard."

"That's right."

"That's horrible! Laytana needs to find those creeps and punish them. Did you tell her?"

"What is she going to do? I can't identify them. I never saw their faces. And besides, if I told Laytana two jerks attacked me because I was investigating Jodie's murder, she'd lock *me* up, not them."

"Did you recognize their voices?"

"They never said a word. Maybe I've met them before, and that's why they didn't speak. But they were a good team. They knew what to do, and they got right to it."

"Ernest, you better stay in your cabin for the rest of the trip. You're not safe walking around."

Jackson made his usual post-show appearance. "Fantastic show, you two! The concerts just kept getting better and better each night. Tonight the merchandise flew off the table. We ran out of the CDs and tapes."

"Hear that, Sis? Your music is a hot seller."

She beamed. "Wow. I never expected that."

Frank stepped into the room. "The band's having a last-show, end-of-the-tour celebration party in the bar."

I said, "You guys use any excuse to party, don't you?"

"Are you coming, Sandy?"

"Afraid I'll have to pass, Frank. Doctor's orders." When I sent word to the band about the first show's cancellation, I said that I'd taken ill, not that I'd fallen into the sea. Trying to explain the situation was something I needed to do in person, not through the grapevine.

"Sorry to hear that, Sandy. How are you feeling?"

"Better but tired, thanks. What time will you be packing up the gear?"

"Right after lunch tomorrow," said Frank. "I doubt that the guys will be up any earlier."

"Fine. I'll meet with everyone then, and we'll debrief the shows."

"Can I go party with the band?" Celeste asked. "I'm too excited to go to bed."

"Sure, knock yourself out. I'll be asleep when you return, so don't wake me. Frank, tell the guys to behave like gentlemen around my sister."

We all said our goodbyes. Celeste took Frank's arm, and they cleared my dressing room. As much as I wanted one last chance to hang out with the guys, who'd been super all week, I was fading fast. I barely had enough energy to make it back to the suite.

I'd wiped off the last of the makeup when Cinnamon knocked. "Hi, Sandy. I was afraid I'd miss you. You're the only one still here."

"The others headed for the bar. You know how musicians are."

"I wanted to return these to you." She placed my keycard and wallet on the table beside me. "I found these on the jogging track this afternoon."

"Thank you. They must have fallen out of my pocket when I was fighting with my would-be killers."

"Good thing I found them, or I might not have seen you in the water."

"So you're the one who came to my rescue? You saved

my life, Cinny. I owe you one."

She blushed and waved aside my praise. "You don't owe me anything. How was your show tonight? I'm sorry I missed it, but Garvin wanted to go to the piano bar so we could talk things over."

"And did you? Talk things over, I mean?"

"He did most of the talking. I listened."

"What did he talk about?"

She looked hurt. "Nothing that concerns you."

"Cinny, come in please and close the door. I need to tell you something."

She did so and sat in the chair Celeste had just vacated. Delicacy was never my strong point, so I got to the point. "I think Garvin is involved with the robberies onboard the ship." She opened her mouth to reply but I held up a hand. "No, wait, hear me out." I summarized my afternoon adventure with Garvin atop the Water Tower.

As I expected, the news did not please her. "Of course Garvin had every right to be angry with you, the way you were stalking him."

"People don't hightail it across town unless they're guilty of something."

"Sandy, first you tell me that two mystery men threw you off the ship. Then you have the gall to say Garvin tried to push you off a tower. Have you always been so paranoid? That sort of thing doesn't happen to people except in the movies."

"What about him selling the necklace?"

"That was one of the things Garvin explained to me. He said he was going to use the money to buy me some jewelry that I liked. If I had wanted the emerald necklace, he would have given me the real one when we returned home. He didn't feel it was safe for me to carry it while we were traveling."

"I think Garvin had something to do with Jodie's death."

She slapped me across the cheek. Her green eyes flashed. "How dare you call him a killer!"

"I didn't say he was the one who strangled her. But he's involved somehow."

"That's a monstrous thing to stay!" She stood. "Goodnight, Sandy." The way she spoke, the words dripped venom.

"Wait, Cinny—"

"It's time for you to stop playing boy sleuth." Tears welled in her eyes. "You're a terrible detective. You have no idea how to find a killer. All you're doing is hurting people."

Cinnamon slammed the door behind her, leaving me alone with my unproven theories and the realization that I'd just alienated the girl I loved.

FRIDAY: At Sea
Chapter 18: A Little Less Conversation

As the ship headed back to homeport, I settled in for a day of relaxation in the suite. My assailants probably knew that I was still alive and would no doubt make another attempt on my life, so I planned to stay off the Lido Deck until we disembarked in Fort Lauderdale. Celeste and I both slept in late. On waking, I changed the bandages on my hands. For breakfast I called room service for cinnamon rolls (after my harrowing escape yesterday, I deserved a treat), juice, coffee and—at my sister's request—two of the ship's specialty drinks, the Favorable Forecast (virgin for me). Clad in swimsuits, sunglasses and suntan lotion, we sprawled in the lounge chairs on my private balcony and ate a leisurely breakfast as we watched the wake churn.

"Sis, are you going to keep that hairdo?"

"For a while. I like it, and I don't have to brush my hair every day." She swung her hair until the braids flew every which way. I think she liked doing that.

"Don't stand close to anyone when you do that, or those beads will put their eye out."

"What do you think our parents will say when they see my hair?"

"Mother will love it. Father will have a heart attack."

Celeste played with the little umbrella in her drink glass. "I see you managed to stay sober for a whole week."

"You sound disappointed."

"I didn't think you could do it."

"How do you know I didn't nip a little when you

weren't around?"

"I can smell alcohol on you."

Maybe my sister can't see, but she's aware of everything. "Thanks for that vote of confidence."

"Don't get me wrong. I like you better when you're sober."

"I like me better too."

"Do you miss it? Drinking, I mean?"

I took a sip of my virgin drink. "I miss the social part, sitting down with someone for a drink. I hate having to explain myself when people ask. But no, I don't miss what booze did to me."

"After all these years, why did you stop drinking?"

"Because of Becka."

"Your ex-wife? I thought you weren't speaking to her."

"We're talking now. Barely. Anyway, Becka said I couldn't see my kids again until I sobered up and started working."

"Sorry I asked."

"No, I should have told you. Anyway, it was the kick in the pants I needed to restart my life."

"I haven't seen my niece and nephew in a long time."

"I know. When we get home, I'll try to set up a visit. Escaping that watery grave yesterday was easier than trying to pry my kids out of Becka's clutches."

"Warren brings his kids around all the time to see me."

Couldn't I have just one week pass without someone reminding me how my spectacular brother always surpassed my meager efforts? "That's nice."

Some seagulls flew overhead. A moment of silence passed before my sister spoke. "Those men who threw you overboard yesterday. Did you notice anything about them? Cologne, body odor, mannerisms?"

Of course, I needed a blind person to remind me of the things I often overlooked. "At the time, I was so busy thinking about survival I didn't stop and take notes. Wait a minute. I do remember something unusual. One of the guys who attacked me was a woman."

"A woman? You said you didn't see their faces."

"That's right, but women have other attributes. The person who tied my hands had a nice pair of jugs."

"Ernest, is that the first thing you notice about a woman?" She sounded exasperated.

"One of the first, yes. I mean, she was sitting on my chest. *Her* chest was right in my face, and she had on a snug tee shirt. How could I miss it?"

"I can understand why a woman would be mad enough to throw you overboard."

"I just stuck out my tongue at you."

Celeste replied likewise.

The increased noise from the Lido Deck overhead caught my attention. "What's the time?"

She checked her Braille watch. "Eleven-forty."

Our luncheon date with the fans! I told Celeste we had to dress and head over to the Aries Dining Room pronto. We showed up fashionably late at five after twelve. The fans had squeezed in two extra chairs around their already-cramped round table. Bunny made sure she sat beside me. Most of the fans I already knew; I'd either met them earlier this week or at my previous gigs at the Beatles convention or the sitcom. The diehard fans tended to turn up repeatedly, so after a while I recognized their faces. I was so busy answering questions about my glory days that I didn't have a chance to eat. Occasionally, someone asked Celeste a direct question. That was the only time she talked, because she was concentrating on not making a mess while eating.

Out of curiosity about the other performers, I asked if anyone had seen the other shows.

"I did!" said Trish. "I saw the big revue in the

showroom. The singing and dancing were great. Not as good as you, Sandy, but pretty good."

"Yeah, I saw that one too," said Barbara. "I liked the magician the best. He was an escape artist. He got out of chains and handcuffs. They locked him into a big trunk and when they opened it, he was gone! Then the girl on stage pointed out that he was sitting in the back row of the theater. That was neat."

"I saw the ventriloquist," said Mary. "His dummy was a real smart aleck. They had a routine about 'how to commit the perfect murder.' The dummy, his name was Moze, said the trick was to dump the body in someone else's house so it looked like they did it. And the ventriloquist said he was going to tie a rope around Moze's neck and drop him off in somebody's cabin tonight!"

"I hope he doesn't leave the dummy in my room!" I tried to make a joke of it, but despite my smile, I felt uneasy. That scenario sounded a little too familiar.

"The guy in the piano bar was so-so," said Jill. "He seemed kind of distracted, like he couldn't wait to finish and run off."

"Yeah, and who was that nasty-looking bleached blonde who sat beside him all night?" said Bertha. "Wasn't she a trashy dresser!"

Tommy never mentioned to me that he had a girlfriend. Who was this new female fatale?

We finished eating, and the girls thanked me profusely for spending time with them. I, in turn, thanked them for their loyalty. Sure, fans can get gushy and a bit too clingy, but they're the ones who kept the spark flickering in my career.

Celeste and I left the dining room. "Where to now?" she asked as we headed for the elevator.

"I'm going back to the room. I've had enough adventure this week."

"I want to see more of the ship."

"Do you think that's wise, after what happened to me yesterday?"

"There's no reason why anyone would want to hurt me, is there?"

She had a point. Only the people who came to our shows knew about our relationship. Celeste had never met Jodie, and she knew even less about the murder than I did.

"No, I suppose not," I said. "Are you sure you won't get lost?"

"I know my way around. I went over the layout this morning while you were still in bed. I can handle it."

"Okay. Be back by six so we can have dinner and get dressed. Tonight's the costume party."

"I can't wait! It'll be fun."

With cane in hand, she set out on her own. I retired to the cabin to lie on the bed and watch a movie. But partway into the film, my mind wandered, and I turned off the TV. I stared at the ceiling and pondered. We were in the final day of the cruise, and I still hadn't solved Jodie's murder. Sure, I had plenty of suspects, but no solid evidence to nail the right one. My fingers itched to phone Laytana and see if she had any leads, but she'd only accuse me of interfering. I wondered if the security officer was simply going to let the murderer escape to avoid bad publicity for the cruise line. Once the ship docked tomorrow morning, the killer would be home free.

A loud beeping sound interrupted my contemplation. In my drowsiness I couldn't place the noise—it didn't sound like the phone, and the room didn't have a doorbell. The noise came from the two-way radio on the table. I'd forgotten about that thing. Celeste must have gotten lost after all and needed direction. I'd have to tease her later about her overconfidence.

I picked up the radio and pushed the transmission

button. "Hey, Sis, what's up?"

She sounded terrified. "Help me!"

Chapter 19: All Shook Up

I'd never heard her so scared. "Sis? Where are you?"
She started to cry. "Calm down. I can't understand you if
you're blubbering. Tell me where you are."

"I don't know."

"Are you lost?"

"A man, he grabbed me and shoved me into a box."

Now she had my full attention. "A man? What man?"

"I don't know."

The same sadist who tried to drown me had gone after
my sister. I paced the room as I talked, trying to listen. The
signal kept cutting in and out. "You have to speak clearly. I
can barely hear you over the static. Are you in the box
now?"

"No."

"Good. Is the man still there?"

"No. I think he's gone."

"Listen, I'm coming for you, but I need you to guide me.
What deck are you on?"

"I don't know."

"Sis! Concentrate! What's the last place you remember?
Were you in the lounge, the casino, the pool, where?"

"I heard music. Piano music. I was by a room with piano
music."

I rummaged around on the desk and found the brochure
with a map of the ship's interior. "That must be the Pisces
Piano Bar. That's on the Astrology Deck. Good. That
helps. After you heard the music, did you use the stairs or
the elevator?"

"No, I don't think so. Ernest, I'm scared. Please hurry."

"I'm trying." The information narrowed her location to one deck, but that level had plenty of rooms. "Where did the man grab you? Were you actually in the piano bar?"

"No."

I rubbed my forehead. The radio's battery was running low, and her voice was fading. "Can you describe the room where you are now?" I heard her walking and crashing into things. "Be careful. Use your cane."

"I lost it when the man grabbed me."

"What are you bumping into?"

"Boxes. Big boxes. Crates."

"Like trunks? Packing trunks?"

"Yeah, I think so."

"Hang on. Stay put, and don't move. I know where you are. I'm on my way."

I threw down the radio, grabbed my keycard and wallet—in my panic I picked up my wallet without thinking—and ran, not walked, up the crew stairs to the Astrology Deck. I had no time to wait for the elevator. I headed to the backstage area behind the Sagittarius Showroom. Of all the venues, the showroom had the largest backstage area in which to keep the numerous costumes and props for the show, and all of those items needed storage boxes. And it was also the only large storage accessible by non-crewmembers. I couldn't imagine a crewman risking his job to hurt my sister. In the hallway behind the showroom stage, I found my sister's cane on the floor. I was on the right track. I folded the cane and stuck it into the waistband of my pants. I passed several dressing rooms and found a room marked "Storage"—and a secured door. The villain wasn't about to let Celeste escape.

I pounded on the door. "Sis? Are you in there?" I thought I heard a muffled voice, but with the air conditioning whooshing through the overhead vent I couldn't be sure.

A maid shuffled down the hallway, pushing a clothes rack filled with freshly laundered costumes—pantsuits covered with fringe and sequins—for use in the revue.

"Hello!" I flashed my famous smile at her. "Can you please help me? I need to get to my trunk, but the door's locked."

She smiled and nodded. "Yes, the door is always locked."

"You don't understand. I accidentally left my best suit in my trunk before I put it away. In my suit pocket there's an engagement ring. I was going to propose to my girlfriend tonight on the Lido Deck under the moonlight. So you see, I have to get to my trunk."

She nodded again. "But nobody goes in the room without permission of the stage manager."

To speed the transaction, I fished a twenty-dollar bill from my wallet—how lucky I had that with me—and slipped the money into her hand. "I'd really appreciate any help you can give me. I can't propose without a ring."

She stuffed the bribe into her apron pocket, pulled a master keycard from her pocket, and unlocked the door.

I gave her a wink. "You won't tell anyone about this, will you? I wouldn't want to spoil the surprise for my girlfriend."

"Just close the door when you finish. Stage manager, he will be angry if the door is left open." She kicked a wooden wedge beneath the door. "The door will lock automatically when you close it."

"Thank you so much." I kissed her cheek.

She giggled and left the rack of clothes standing outside the door as she walked off. I stepped into the pitch-black room. I felt for a wall switch and turned it on. Light flooded the space. Crates, racks, boxes and suitcases filled the small room.

"Celeste? It's me, Ernest. Are you in here?"

I heard sobbing to my left. I inched my way through the narrow spaces between the boxes. She sat on the floor, back against the wall, her knees drawn up and arms wrapped around her legs. She was crying buckets.

I knelt beside her. She raised her head with a start. "It's me, Ernest."

"Ernest!" She flung her arms around me and cried.

I held her and patted her on the back. "Hush, it's okay. You're safe. You said this man put you in a box?"

"Uh huh."

Crates of all sizes surrounded us. "I'm going to stand up and look around. I'm not leaving you."

She clung to me, but I loosened her arms and rose to my feet. Celeste wouldn't have moved far from where she was held captive. Only one box in the vicinity was large enough to hold a person. One side was open. As I inspected the inside of the crate, I caught a flash of light out of the corner of my eye. Something on the floor reflected the light from the fluorescent ceiling tubes. I bent over, took out my handkerchief, and used it to pick up a small, shiny object. Ah ha! The clue I needed to catch the killer. Most of my suspects had lost a polished item this week. I wrapped the cloth around the object and stuck it in my pants' pocket.

Footsteps and voices drifted in from the hallway. If someone noticed the open door, they'd close it, trapping both of us inside.

I grabbed Celeste's hands and pulled her to her feet. "We've got to get out of here, now."

I put one arm around her shoulder to hurry her along. At the doorway, I peeked out. Hugh and Mindy were headed our way. They were engrossed in conversation and not looking in our direction—for now. Where could we hide? The door across the hallway might be locked. Our only chance was the rack of clothes left by the maid. I snapped off the wall switch and pushed Celeste out the door. We squeezed in between the clothes rack and the wall.

She started to speak. "Ernest, what—"

I clapped a hand over her mouth. "Don't make a sound." With my other hand, I held her tight against me. I couldn't see Mindy and Hugh, but I heard them stop on the other side of the clothes rack. I held my breath. Would they notice our feet below the hanging clothes? Couldn't they hear my pounding heartbeat?

"Do we have to get rid of them?" Mindy asked. "They're kind of nice people."

"It's for the good of the show," he replied. "They've caused too much damage already."

"Well, okay."

"Who left this door open? I've harped at the cast and crew a million times about leaving this door ajar. We'd get sued if something was stolen."

The door slammed shut and our interlopers moved on. I let out a sigh of relief and dropped my hand from my sister's mouth. I peeked out from among the hanging clothes—all clear. I took Celeste's hand, and we ran down the hall. We bolted down the crew stairs two at a time. In our haste, Celeste stumbled a couple of times, and I caught her. In the safety of my stateroom, I set her on the bed and bolted the door shut.

"Okay, Sis, we're in my cabin. Nobody can hurt you now."

She wept tears of relief. I placed the ship's complimentary box of tissues in her hand. I also gave her a glass of water, which she drank. I removed the cane from my pants and the fanny pack from her waist—and noticed something was missing.

"Where's the radio?" I asked.

"The radio? Isn't it in my pack?"

"No."

"I guess I dropped it after I called you. I was upset. I'm sorry."

"Don't worry about it. I didn't mark the radio with your name, so nobody can link it to you. Anyway, with all the clutter in the storage room, I doubt that anyone will see it."

"What if the killer calls you on the radio?"

"Then we'll know who it is, won't we?"

I sat on the bed with her until she calmed down.

"Ernest, I was so frightened."

"I know. But you were very brave. You didn't lose your head. Can you tell me what happened?"

She blew her nose and wiped her eyes. "I was walking down the hall. A man said hello. He said he saw our show and he thought I was wonderful."

"Did you recognize his voice?" She shook her head. "You're sure it was a man, not a woman."

She nodded. "He asked if I needed help. I said I wanted to go to the place where the piano music was playing. I could hear the music from the hall. He said he'd take me there. We walked a long way, and I didn't hear any music. I said, 'This isn't the right place. Where are we?' He opened a door and pushed me into a room. I fought him. I tried to get away. He said he was going to kill me if you didn't stop poking about into Jodie's death."

"The sleazebag."

She continued. "And he shoved me into a box and locked it."

"How did you get out if it was locked?"

"I don't know. I beat on the sides and called for help. I felt around to try to find a way out. All of a sudden, the side popped open. Then I called you on the radio."

"This time I'm telling Laytana. Nobody kidnaps my sister and lives to tell the tale." I picked up the phone and started dialing.

"Ernest."

"What is it?"

"I saw his face."

My dialing finger froze. "You did what?"

"When he put me in the box, I tried to push him away, and I touched his face."

I hung up the phone. "Can you describe what he looks like?"

"I think so. Why?"

"I have an idea. I'm going to bring someone here. You're going to describe the man, and she'll draw a picture, like a police sketch. I can show that drawing to Laytana and maybe she can identify the man."

"There isn't a police artist on board."

"We've got the next best thing. Trust me on this. I'll be right back. Go to your room. Don't answer the phone. Don't open to door to anyone, not even the maid. Got it?"

I made sure the door to Celeste's room was locked tight and bolted. I placed the "do not disturb" sign on the outside knob. Finding the person I needed would be easy. She wasn't the type to spend her time in the casino or bars. Where would a person from the rainy, overcast Midwest spend her time on a sunny tropical day? As I expected, I found her topside beside the pool along with some of her friends. My fan club waved and greeted me as I approached.

I said, "Hi, girls, are you having fun?"

"Yeah, Sandy," said Trish. "This cruise is the most fun ever!"

"Bunny, can I see you for a minute?"

"Sure, Sandy, what is it?"

I motioned for her to come to me. Bunny put on a short terrycloth robe over her one-piece swim suit, picked up her Yellow Submarine tote bag and beach towel, and shuffled over to me. She wore flip-flops, dark clip-on lenses over her glasses, and a wide-brim floppy white hat. I stepped away from the group of women so the others wouldn't overhear.

"Bunny, I need your help. Can you get your drawing pad and pencils right away?"

"I got them with me. They're in my bag."

"Good. I need you to draw a picture for me. It's very important. I'll explain later."

She looked puzzled but followed me anyway to my sister's room. Normally, I had strict rules about not letting fans into my hotel rooms. But this was an emergency, and Bunny was the one fan I could trust. I set out chairs for Bunny and my sister.

"Sis, this is Bunny McAllister. You met her at the shows."

"Hi, Celeste!," said Bunny. "Wow, you sure have a nice cabin. Mine's two decks below, just a tiny thing with no windows."

"Bunny, my sister is going to describe a man to you. I need you to draw his face."

"I've never done that before, Sandy. I have to look at something when I draw it."

"So you're going to learn a new skill. Expand your talents. We need a picture of this man."

"Is he a bad man?"

"A very bad man."

"I'll do my best."

Bunny set up her pad on her lap. With pencil in hand, she began a rough sketch as Celeste talked. This would take some time. My presence would probably distract Bunny, so I walked up one level to the Constellation Deck. I hadn't spent time here—not much to see on this deck except the Cancer Shopping Plaza with the ship's stores and the photo gallery. Since this was the last day of the cruise, the shops had slashed the prices on the usually overpriced merchandise for clearance, so the deck was crowded with bargain hunters. Good. The assailant would be foolish to attack me in front of so many witnesses.

Numerous pictures taken by the ship's photographers lined the hallway—all prints for sale, of course. I found some nice shots of Celeste and myself. Our parents would enjoy those. I noticed another pix, a candid shot taken in the atrium. I wasn't in the photo, but certain other people were visible in the background. I bought a print of that shot as well.

By the time I returned, Bunny had finished her sketch. "I'm not sure this is accurate, but see what you think."

I took the sketch from her and grinned. "Bunny, you did very well."

I knew this face. I held the last piece of evidence I needed to nail Jodie's killer.

I thanked Bunny and sent her on her way with orders to keep this incident a secret. I finally made that call to Laytana and explained my theory.

"That's all very interesting, Mr. Fairfax, but hardly convincing. You are not a sworn law enforcement officer. Your friend is not a police sketch artist. You don't have a warrant. I'm afraid your so-called evidence wouldn't count for much."

"Can you at least question the suspect? Maybe you can beat a confession out of them."

"If the person is innocent, the cruise line may be sued for harassment."

How did this woman ever get a job in security?

"Laytana, I have an idea. Tonight's the costume gala. I'm positive the suspect will show up. What if I smoke them out? I can put on a big show that I'm going to reveal the killer's identity. If it's the right person, you can make an arrest. If not, then I'm the one who looks like an idiot, and the cruise line is off the hook."

"The passengers are supposed to have a good time at

these parties, not be subjected to a police investigation."

"I'll make believe it's a parlor game, like Colonel Mustard in the kitchen with the candlestick. The guests will think it's all in pretend fun."

"Mr. Fairfax, you're crazy."

"I know that. Laytana, I'm going to do this with or without your support, so unless you plan to put me under house arrest, I'll be at that gala tonight, and I'm going to unmask the killer."

I hung up before she could object.

Chapter 20: (You're The) Devil In Disguise

After Celeste's unpleasant experience, she preferred to dine in the safety of our suites. I insisted she'd feel after a bite, so I ordered some of her favorite foods: smoked honey ham, mac and cheese, and bean salad, as well as a glass of wine to help calm her nerves. We ate at the table inside my suite lest our mutual foe attempt to drop down on us from the Lido Deck. Over dinner, I discussed my thoughts on the murderer's identity and, for once, Celeste didn't poke holes in my theory, which meant I must be right.

When we finished eating, I said. "Sis, I'd really like for you to come with me to the gala and give me moral support. I understand you might still be scared about going out in public, so I won't push you. I have to go and face the killer. I have no choice, but you do. You can join me or stay here for the evening. It's up to you."

She bent her head down and absently toyed with her napkin, deep in thought. "I'll go. I'm tired of these bullies pushing me around."

"Atta, girl."

"But you better not leave me alone."

"I'll stick to you like the paparazzi. I'll even follow you into the ladies' room."

"I don't think you could get away with that."

"Just watch me."

She smiled. "Besides, I want to show off my costume."

Don't ask me why we had decided to go as Robin Hood and Maid Marian. Celeste just wanted to get me into tights, which I loathe. I told her I did not have to suffer with those itchy, chaffing things just because Douglas Fairbanks wore tights in a movie. Normally, finding costumes in Los Angeles right before Halloween was impossible, but I had connections. Mammoth Picture Studio, where I had filmed my TV show, rented clothing from its vast storehouse to other productions. I called the wardrobe manager, who knew me well, and she helped to find outfits for both of us.

My togs consisted of loose brown pants tucked into brown leather knee boots; a short-sleeve green tunic over a cream-colored shirt with long, puffy sleeves; a brown leather belt; brown cape and a green hat with real pheasant feathers. I removed the bandages from my palms, which were still sore but healing. I had a brown leather pouch on my belt, which I used to store Bunny's face sketch, the purchased photo and the shiny object I'd found in the storage room. Robin Hood was now a sleuth.

Celeste, as usual, looked like a vision in her garb: a long, patterned blue dress and an embroidered ribbon belt with the ends hanging down the front. The dress sleeves ended at the elbow and then hung down, revealing the silver lining. The modest neckline (Celeste didn't like to show her cleavage) and around the elbows were lined with embroidered ribbon to match the belt. She had blue slippers, sparkling rhinestone jewelry and circlet with a long veil on her head.

"The braids look a bit out of character," I said.

"I'm making my own fashion statement."

"That you are. You look gorgeous."

"Help me with the gauntlets, please?"

I laced up the white satin gauntlets on her forearms. Celeste insisted on wearing her dark glasses (the specs made her feel less vulnerable in public), so I was spared the chore of applying her makeup. After my altercation with Cinnamon last night, I was afraid to ask her for any favors.

"Wait, I need to pick up one more item," I said.

"What's that?"

"My bow and arrows."

"You actually brought along a bow and arrows?"

"How can I be Robin Hood without a bow and arrows?"

"Let me see."

I placed an arrow in her hand. "Careful, don't touch the point. It's sharp."

The studio prop department had loaned me a breakaway bow (for easy packing in a suitcase) and a leather quiver full of period arrows. The points were real arrowheads, not rubber suction cups or blunt tips. Studio props are quite authentic.

"The studio trusts you with sharp objects?" she teased.

"See, you have nothing to worry about. I'm armed. I can protect you."

"You couldn't hit the side of the ship with these arrows."

"Can to. I had to learn archery for my show. I hit the target most of the time without using camera tricks."

"Your stunt double did the shooting."

"He did not! The guy who taught me made me practice for hours."

I hoisted the quiver's strap and the bow over one shoulder and let Celeste take my arm. As we headed for the elevator, she clung to me more for protection than guidance. Instead of sweeping her cane in front, she clutched it as a defensive weapon.

The Cosmic Atrium was decorated as befitting a Halloween party: streamers of twinkling black-and-orange lights, hanging metal cutouts of black cats and white ghosts, spider-web tablecloths and real jack-o'-lanterns on the floor, courtesy of the "carve a pumpkin" contest earlier that day. The black night sky, visible through the skylight, added an appropriately sinister touch to the proceedings. On a portable platform set up along a wall, a DJ spun suitable music such as "Monster Mash," "Time Warp," "Witch Doctor" and the "Ghostbusters" theme, along with various spooky sound effects such as creaky doors and maniacal laughter.

The atrium lights were dimmed. A mobile spotlight roamed over the crowd, stopping for a moment on some of the more memorable costumes. Of course, an Elvis or two in white sequined jumpsuits showed up along with the usual witches, goblins, Frankenstein's monsters and vampires. In honor of the ship's name, some creative souls dressed up as astrology signs; someone asked if I was dressed as Sagittarius, the Archer.

My fan club found me right away. "Hey, Sandy, I love what you're wearing!" said Bunny. She was decked out as a Southern belle complete with hoop skirt, a lace fan and white lace gloves. "That's exactly like the outfit you wore on the episode 'The Shady Sherwood Forest Caper.'"

"Is it?"

Celeste and I spent about twenty minutes posing for snapshots with every one of my costumed fans who came armed with a camera. All part of the job. After that, Celeste and I made our way to one of the food and beverage stands to get a drink. She'd already had a couple of drinks today, so I picked up a cup of "blood red" cranberry punch for each of us. I spotted Cinnamon and Garvin, dressed as Cleopatra and Mark Antony. Cinnamon was, of course, stunning as ever in a sleeveless white gown. Metal snakes coiled around her upper arms. She had a crown on her head, wide jeweled bracelets around her wrists and also a scarab necklace—no doubt another fake from her shyster boyfriend. She'd painted her face in the stylized Egyptian manner with heavy eyeliner and dark eye shadow. Garvin was in a Roman soldier's outfit with a metal breastplate, skirt and sandals laced to the knee. I hoped he wasn't planning to use that realistic-looking metal sword strapped around his waist.

Cinnamon and I locked eyes for a moment. She turned her head and moved away before I could say hello. Celeste and I mingled briefly with the band members before I caught up with Laytana.

"Mr. Fairfax, Miss Farmington, how nice you both look tonight." Laytana, ever the party pooper, was still in her uniform. I almost made a crack about her coming to the party disguised as a security officer, but that would have me arrested. "Does that costume mean you're planning some derring-do?"

"That's where I need your help," I said. "After I smoke out the killer, my guess is the culprit will make a run for it. If you could put your security officers at the exits—"

"Mr. Fairfax, there are several hundred people here. I do not intend for you to start a stampede that will endanger the guests."

"Laytana, if we just sit pretty tonight, tomorrow morning the murderer will walk off this ship home free. Do you want that on your conscience?"

"What I don't want is a ship full of injured and panicked passengers."

One of the other passengers asked Laytana a question. I used the distraction to hurry away with Celeste in tow. And who did we bump into but Aaron and Moze, who were dressed in tuxedos as Edger Bergen and Charlie McCarthy. The dummy even sported a top hat and monocle.

"Well, look who showed up armed and ready!" said Moze. "Is the meat on this ship so rotten you have to shoot your own?"

"Hush up, Moze, or I'll carve some arrows out of you," I quipped.

"Ouch! I get the point."

Aaron said, "Hello, Sandy, Celeste. How do you like the party?"

"That sounds like Aaron," she said.

"That's right," I said.

"Hello, Aaron," she replied. "We only just got here."

"I think this gig is going to heat up in a bit," I said. "I'm planning on unmasking Jodie's killer tonight."

"Really?" Aaron sounded scared. "How do you know who it is?"

"You'll see."

I watched his face for a reaction. He muttered something about having to meet someone and slipped away. Aaron must have been rattled if he left without Moze making a parting insult.

Hugh and Mindy were having a grand old time beside one of the drink stations. Both held a flute of champagne. From their raucous laughter, I doubted it was their first glass. She was dolled up in a short fringed dress and long beads as a Roaring '20s flapper. His zoot suit with the wide lapels and pinstripes, along with the baggy pants and fedora, must have come straight out of the wardrobe closet for *Guys and Dolls*.

Robert Markson, the poor slob in Jodie's blackmail photos, and his wife each had a wine glass in hand as they mingledg among the guests. I pursed my lips to keep from laughing out loud at their choice of costume: Early American Puritans, with a black dress and white apron and kerchief for her, and a black jacket with a large white collar, short black pants, white hose, black shoes and a black conical hat for him. After his fling with Jodie, this esteemed executive certainly wasn't living the austere life of a Puritan.

Someone tapped my shoulder from behind. "Well, well. And who are you supposed to be?"

I turned to face Tommy, "Can't you guess? The bow and arrows should be a clue."

"I see. Robin Hood. How pedestrian. I expected

something more from you, Fairfax."

"Like what, a gorilla suit? I'm not one of the Monkees."

He laughed. "All right, then, who am I?"

"An eighteenth-century French fop?"

It seemed like a good guess considering his white powdered curled wig, a velvet waistcoat over a white ruffled suit, ornate coat, knee-length breeches, white hose and buckled shoes.

He frowned. "You call yourself a musician and you don't recognize Wolfgang Amadeus Mozart?"

"Maybe if you hummed a few bars from *The Marriage of Figaro*."

"Ha, ha, always the cut-up. Are you enjoying this drab excuse of a party? I wouldn't recommend refilling your glass. Toward the end of the cruise, the liquor runs low, and the staff starts watering the drinks."

"Thanks, but I don't intend to get loaded. I need a clear head for tonight."

"May I ask why? Are you planning an assignation with a young lady?"

"I'm going to identify Jodie's killer."

The smile dropped off his face. "How amusing. And I thought Aaron was the resident comedian."

"I'm serious."

"I don't doubt it." He leaned in close to my face. "A word of warning, Fairfax. It's almost Halloween, and the evil spirits are out. I wouldn't expect the murderer to go into custody without putting up a fight."

"Do you know something I don't?"

Before Tommy could answer, a costumed couple approached—Rex and his daughter.

"Good evening, Rex," said the pianist. "That outfit suits you."

"That fancy dress of yours would get you arrested at the Grand Ole Opry," Rex replied. "I say, Sandy, you're looking dapper. I hope you aren't planning on using those arrows tonight. Do you have someone in your sights?"

"He's going to tell us who killed Jodie," said Tommy.

Rex arched an eyebrow ever so slightly. "Really? And who would that be?"

I said, "Now, Rex, as a magician, you know I can't reveal my secrets."

Nessie tugged on her father's sleeve. "Daddy, let's go. This party is a bore."

"Nonsense, my little petunia," he said. "Sounds like things are just getting interesting. I wouldn't miss this for all the corn in Kansas."

Tommy said, "If you'll all excuse me. I see a lady friend that I must talk to." With that, he slipped away into the crowd.

Celeste said to me, "Ernest, is this really such a good idea? What if you're wrong about the killer?"

Just then, the Zodiac's entertainment director stepped up on the platform and stood at the microphone stand. While she gabbed on and on, I set my cup on a table, took my sister's hand and maneuvered to the edge of the stage.

"I'm going up on the platform. I need you to sit down until I'm finished."

"No! You said you wouldn't leave me alone!

"I have to do this."

"I'm going with you."

"Sis, I—"

"What if the killer grabs me as a hostage while you're busy?"

"All right, but at least let me do the talking."

"As if I could stop you."

We waited until the emcee finished awarding the prizes for the costume contest (Celeste and I should have won, but I had other things on my mind). I helped Celeste step onto the platform. Then I asked the emcee for the mic; she was surprised to see me. At my onstage appearance, my fan club instantly gathered in front of the stage, always ready to see me in action. I hoped they were not placing themselves in the way of danger.

The emcee announced, "Ladies and gentlemen, Sandy Fairfax!"

I took the mic out of the stand. The people near the stage watched in idle amusement, no doubt thinking I was part of the planned entertainment. Those standing farther away kept chatting and drinking, ignoring me.

The emcee asked, "Sandy, are you going to sing for us?"

"No, but I have something important to say."

I moved to the front of the stage. Celeste stood behind me to my right, the DJ and emcee to my left. My heart beat madly. What was I doing? From the floor, Laytana scowled at me, but what could she do? She'd look stupid hauling me off in front of these people without saying why.

"Hi, folks," I said. "In the spirit of the evening, I'd like to play a real-life game of Clue. During your enjoyable week at sea, you probably didn't hear about the crimes taking place onboard this ship. While you were having fun, some bad guys were behaving very badly. For those of you who may have lost some valuables this week or on previous cruises, I'd like to introduce one of the persons responsible for those shenanigans, Garvin Lee!"

As I expected, he pushed his way to the stage, leaving a stunned Cinnamon behind. He shouted some unsavory language at me. "What are you saying?"

"Don't play dumb, Garvin. The emerald necklace I saw you sell in Nassau was one of the stolen pieces."

"You're insane. I'm not a jewel thief."

"You're right. You don't have the brains or the guts to actually do the stealing. You're only the fence. The real thief would scout out the passengers and spot the most expensive pieces. Before the next cruise, you had glass replicates made. You hawked the stolen loot on the islands so the pieces couldn't be traced. If you were caught, you'd just trot out one of the fake pieces to cover your tail."

Cinnamon made her way next to Garvin. "Is this true?" She sounded more confused than angry.

"He's lying!" Garvin shouted. "He's drunk! It's the booze speaking!"

"I assure you, I'm stone cold sober," I said. "And speaking of stone, it's time to expose the villain who not only tied an iron weight to me for some unwanted deep sea diving, but also kidnapped my sister and murdered Jodie Russ. May I present this all-around scoundrel and the Zodiac's resident jewel thief—Rex Stevenford!"

By now, I had the rapt attention of the entire crowd. A collective gasp ran among the guests. The mobile spotlight fell on Rex, the handsome devil (how appropriate). He was garbed as Mephistopheles, in a long red robe and cape, red hood and slippers. His face had a black pointed fake beard, moustache and slanted bushy eyebrows. He clutched a metal trident in his gloved hands. Nessie, standing beside him, portrayed a pretty she-devil in red tights and leotard with a pointed tail and a red hood with horns.

Rex laughed. "I say, Fairfax, that's about the wildest tall tale I've heard in a coon's age!"

"It's time to retire the cowboy act, Rex. If you're a Texan, then I'm a brain surgeon. Like everything about your magic act, Rex Stevenford is an illusion. My guess is you made up this good ol' boy persona because you're on the run from the law."

A scowl replaced his smirk. "Now, boy, you better cough up some proof for these accusations before I sue you for slander."

"Working on a cruise ship gave you access to wealthy victims who wouldn't report the thefts. They'd rather accept an insurance payment for their stolen jewels than drag their names into a public investigation. As an escape artist, you knew how to pick locks and crack safes. To enter the rooms, you pulled a sleight of hand and lifted a passkey from someone—the same way you stole my keycard Monday night. You then passed off the loot to Garvin here," I gestured at the man, "who sold the goods with his jeweler connections."

"Who? I don't know this man."

"Really?" I fished the photo from my pouch. "One of the ship's photographers took this photo in the hallway near the casino. It's date-stamped for Tuesday this week. In the background you can see two men talking as if they knew each other well. We can have the photo enlarged for detail, but the two men look like you and Garvin."

"I met lots of folks during the week. Maybe he was just asking me for the time of day."

"Or the time of your next burglary. But let's move on to the diva's murder. Folks, you didn't see Jodie Russ in the revue this week because Rex murdered her Monday night."

"Now that's a bald-faced lie!" All traces of his Southern drawl vanished.

"Careful, Rex, your accent's slipping. Not only did you kill Jodie, but you and your daughter tried to drown me on Thursday, and today you threatened my sister."

"How would your sister know me? The woman's blind."

I held up Bunny's sketch, a near-perfect likeness of the magician. "Celeste felt your face when you attacked her. This is how she described her attacker."

"That proves nothing. The person who drew that saw my magic act and sketched my face from memory."

Bunny spoke up. "I never saw this man before, honest. I didn't see any of the other shows on the ship 'cause I was at Sandy's concerts every night."

Rex was undaunted. "If Jodie died Monday night, I have an alibi. I performed my act twice in the showroom. Any number of people saw me backstage and onstage."

"During your act, you're locked inside a trunk," I said. "What do you do between the time you leave the trunk and reappear in the audience? I found one of your trick trunks in the storage room. The boxes have a lever inside. During the show, the side drops open, and you escape through a trap door in the floor. After you left the box during the first show on Monday night, you strangled Jodie in the storage room and stashed the body inside one of your empty trunks. You had to ditch the body, so after your escape during the second show you hid the body inside one of the ship's food delivery carts. You ran down the crew hallway and dumped Jodie in my dressing room, which is right next door to the showroom. Tying one of my scarves around her neck was a nice touch."

"Your tale is circumstantial at best and ludicrous at worse. You need evidence, Fairfax, not conjecture."

"Will this do? I found this in the storage room near your trunk." I held up the shiny object I'd picked up in the storage room: Rex's silver buffalo skull tie holder. "You strangled Jodie with your bolo tie. The size and shape of the tie will match the ligature mark on her neck. When you removed the tie from your neck, the clip fell off."

"I'm in the storage room all the time to inspect the props. That could have fallen any time."

"You told me these tie clips were gifts from your late wife. A man in love doesn't lose a present from his honey—unless he's distracted by murder."

"Motive, you need a motive. Why would I want to kill Jodie? She was the best singer in the revue. You've heard me say so."

"Jodie discovered your burglary scheme. She was trying to blackmail you. But you'd rather have her dead and silent than share in the profits."

During this time, Laytana had been observing me with

interest. Now she spoke into the radio clipped to her shirt. The security officers began moving toward Rex. He spotted them closing in. His lips turned up in an evil grin.

"Very nice tale, Fairfax. But there's an old saying among magicians. Now you see me—" He took some small pellets out of his pocket and wrapped the cape around himself, "—and now you don't."

The pellets he threw on the floor exploded in a loud "poof!" A thick mass of smoke enveloped the magician. Those standing near Rex retreated, coughing from the fumes. The security officers fanned away the smoke with their hands—but Rex had vanished.

Chapter 21: Fools Rush In

And the chase was on.

I leapt off the stage and tore after the rat. The guests parted like the Red Sea to let me through. I knew his destination; Rex didn't have many escape options. The elevators would be too slow. Too many people were blocking the crew stairs. But the long corridor that ran through the ship from bow to stern was nearly deserted, as the guests were either in the atrium or in their cabins, packing. If Rex fled into the casino or disco, he'd be trapped. That left the crew stairs aft, accessible through the dining room or the galley. I ran as fast as I could in the clunky boots. Halfway down the corridor, I caught a glimpse of Rex's fluttering cape as he disappeared into the dining room. I followed.

Inside the Aries room, a crewmember swabbed the floor. "The dining room is closed."

"Shut up and leave!" Rex shouted.

The man dropped the mop and dashed out of the room.

Rex spotted me closing in, and he fled into the galley. Why was I spending my pleasant week at sea chasing bad guys? But with no security officers in sight, somebody had to catch the killer. Although the dining room was deserted, inside the galley the chefs were busy preparing for the midnight buffet.

"Stop that man!" I yelled." He's a murderer!"

Most of the chefs moved out of the way. A couple of hardy souls tried to grab Rex, but he shoved them aside. Any man who could easily pick me up and toss me over a ship's railing was one strong fighter. He passed by the dishwashing station and pushed a pile of plates onto the floor to stop me. The china shattered as it hit the tile floor. I gingerly picked my way through the wreckage, grateful that the broken shards didn't piece through the thick boots. That cost me a little time, but I quickly caught up. At the ovens, Rex grabbed the handles of huge pot of boiling pasta and threw it at me. I jumped aside just in time to miss the plume of hot water. I slipped on the wet floor, but didn't lose my balance. A few pieces of cooked pasta clung to my clothes, but I kept going.

At the vegetable carving station, Rex snatched a knife from one of the chefs and confronted me. "Leave me alone, Fairfax." Not a trace of the drawl.

"An innocent man doesn't run," I countered. The bow on my shoulder was getting in my way, so I held it in my hands. "Give up, Rex, or whoever you are. There's no place for you to go unless you plan to jump overboard and swim."

He lunged at me with the knife. I cracked the hardwood of the bow against his wrist. He dropped the weapon. He swung the trident at me. I ducked and blocked the blow with the bow. We feinted several times, Rex advancing and me retreating until my back hit the wall. Rex lowered his aim and whacked me on the ankle.

The trident was not a plastic toy, but the real deal made of metal. I yelped in pain as Rex scooted away. My ankle throbbed too much for me to run. The cooks hid behind the various cooking stations, too scared to confront a madman. That left a clear, open path between the killer and me. Just ahead of Rex stood the door to the crew stairs that led to the deck and the lifeboats. I had to stop him before he left the galley.

I studied the bow in my hands. My next plan was a long shot, but what did I have to lose. With my left hand, I took an arrow from the quiver and strung it on the bow. I aimed, took a deep breath, and released the arrow.

With a soft "whoosh" the missile flew. The arrowhead embedded itself into the back of Rex's calf. Screaming, he fell forward. On the floor, writhing in pain, he tried to grab the arrow.

"Don't pull it out," I yelled, "or you'll start bleeding."

He screamed obscenities at me as the security officers—finally, at long last—made an appearance. I dropped the bow, sank to floor, and closed my eyes. I moaned and rubbed my injured ankle. Then someone said my name. I opened my eyes. Laytana stood over me, hands on her hips. Was she smiling at me?

"That was some pretty fancy shooting, Mr. Fairfax."

I frowned. "Not really. I was aiming for his back."

* * * * *

Once again, I was hauled off to the infirmary, my shipboard home away from home. Doctor Carpenter, bemused at treating me a second time, determined that my ankle was only badly sprained with no broken bones. He taped up the ankle and gave me a cane to use—just the sort of thing that doesn't fit a teen idol's image. The doctor also treated Rex for the arrow wound. No major damage but Rex, himself an illusion, suffered a massive loss of pride by the fact he'd been outwitted by a mere pop singer.

Rex spent the night in an infirmary bed under the vigilant watch of two security officers. Garvin was placed under house arrest in his cabin until we reached Ft. Lauderdale the next morning where both crooks were handed over to the authorities. Nessie was also nabbed for attempted murder and accessory to murder—she had helped her dear old dad with tying me up and also in disposing of Jodie's body.

Several weeks later, I found out Rex's real name. He was wanted on warrants for burglaries at various homes and jewelry shops. He and Garvin had known each other from grade school. They reconnected a few years ago when Rex was casing Garvin's jewelry shop for a possible heist. Garvin's business was floundering, so he teamed up with Rex for a quick and dirty way to raise some tax-free capital. Although Rex and Nessie were adamant about their innocence, Garvin, coward that he was, agreed to testify against them.

On Thursday, Garvin had returned to the ship after the Water Tower incident and told the two about my suspicions. Rex and Nessie then hid by the restaurant on the Lido Deck, waiting for me. I played into their hands by using the jogging track. Otherwise, Garvin was going to intercept me and find an excuse to steer me over by the railing. Nessie had her Madam Balorinsky costume nearby so she could throw on the clothes and get on the Lido Deck to establish an alibi.

Celeste didn't recognize Rex when he stuffed her into the box because he spoke without his drawl. As for the conversation between Hugh and Mindy that Celeste and I had overheard backstage, they were simply discussing two of the newer dancers who were not working out in the revue. Nothing sinister at all.

But for now, with no desire to return to the ship's Halloween party, I hobbled out onto the Lido Deck. I'd been in my stateroom most of the day and desperately needed to look at something besides walls of neutral paint. Tommy and a dishwater blonde were off in the shadows, deep in a heated conversation about money—had he found someone new to mooch off?

Aaron and Moze, still in their costumes, stood by the railing."Hi, Sandy," the ventriloquist greeted. "Moze likes to come up here at night and see the sky."

"Yeah, those are the only stars I'm ever gonna see aboard this tugboat," the dummy said. "So, Sandy, what happened to your foot? Got it stuck in the wrong cabin door?"

"For your information, I captured Jodie's murderer. Turns out Rex was more of a killer than a cowboy."

"So Rex did it!" said Aaron. "I would have never guessed. Maybe now Jodie can rest in peace. Thank you, Sandy. I'm glad you brought that evil man to justice."

"Sounds like you still like her," I said.

"I never stopped loving her, even after the divorce."

"That bimbo wasn't worth your time," Moze said.

"Aaron, there's something I've been wanting to do all week. May I?" I rapped the head of my cane hard on Moze's wooden noggin. "Be nice to your master and stop talking trash to him, or I'll introduce you to my fireplace."

Moze's jaw dropped, but he didn't make a sound.

Aaron said, "Thanks for that too, Sandy."

"My pleasure."

The duo moved along. I was about to leave the deck when I heard crying. A few yards away I found Cinnamon at the railing, crying.

"What's the matter?" I asked.

She sniffled. "Sandy, you were right about Garvin. How could I have been so blind?"

"He fooled everyone, Cinny."

"I was so mean to you." She looked at me with moist green eyes. "Forgive me?"

"Of course."

I embraced her in a warm hug; she melted into my arms. The moon glowed brightly overhead. The deck was quiet and nearly empty save for a few insomniacs. The water lapped gently against the hull. A gentle wind ruffled the feathers in my hat.

After a moment, she pulled away, but I still held her. "That's a terrific costume."

"Cleopatra and Robin Hood," she said. "They're from

two different eras. If they ever met, it'd never work out."

"Don't worry. They'd think of something."

"I'm glad you were on the cruise, Sandy. You made the week something special."

"Call me Ernest."

The moonglow lit up her face. I couldn't resist. I leaned in for a kiss. She closed her eyes and made no move to stop me . . .

"Sandy! Sandy Fairfax!"

I raised my head and dropped my hands, silently cursing the intruder.

The captain approached and shook my hand. "Thank you for helping us capture the thieves and for solving the murder. Well done, indeed, young man. As a token of our appreciation, the cruise line will be issuing a reward."

"I think Celeste deserves some of that reward, don't you, Ernest?" Cinnamon gave me a sly smile. "After all, if it wasn't for her, you would have never found the tie clip in the storage room."

I opened my mouth to protest, but the captain slapped me on the back. "Excellent idea! We'll issue checks to both you and Miss Farmington. By the way, a number of people have mentioned how much they've enjoyed your fine performances each night. The Zodiac would be pleased to have you back for another cruise and more shows."

I'd rather sing for pennies on Sid Row in downtown L.A. than spend one more night on this wreckage, but I only nodded. The captain walked away, whistling happily.

I said to Cinnamon, "I'm glad somebody remembered why I was on this cruise in the first place. Certainly not so Celeste and I could chase a killer." I slapped my forehead. "Sis! I forgot all about her! I left her alone in the atrium. Cinny, I have to go—"

She grabbed my arm. "Don't fret. She's in good hands."

Cinnamon pointed to a circle of young women seated by

the pool. My fan club was enjoying a snack from the all-night pizzeria. They listened intently as Celeste regaled them with embarrassing anecdotes from my childhood. The gals ate up her words with a spoon. Bunny, of course, scribbled down every word on her pad of paper to share with the world in the next edition of her fanzine.

That's what sisters are for.

SATURDAY: Disembarkment
Chapter 22: Goin' Home

Saturday afternoon found the Farmingtons and their luggage aboard a plane headed to the west coast. Earlier that morning, the band members had packed up their instruments, and Jackson loaded up the rented gear to return. As for the stage costumes that Celeste and I had worn, I took them, just in case we might need them again. Who knows?

I also shredded Jodie's blackmail photos and flushed the pieces down the toilet, hoping the paper didn't clog the pipes. I'm sure Robert would be far happier with the cruise pictures the staff photographer took of him with his wife. To my delight, Cinnamon gave me her home phone number. I couldn't wait to get back to L.A. and call her up. With Garvin out of the picture, I envisioned clear sailing ahead for a new relationship.

In the plane's first class section, I set the cane on the floor, stretched out my legs, and winched in pain as my bum ankle struck the seat in front of me.

"So, Sis, are you glad you made the trip?"

"I had a blast. Except for when Rex stuck me in the box. That wasn't fun. But everything else was fantastic. Except for you going overboard. And getting your ankle smashed. And—"

"Okay, I get the picture."

"I'd forgotten how much I love singing. Maybe we can do some shows when we get home?"

"I don't know. You might have a better chance finding

work in the local clubs than I would. I'm more expensive. Besides, most venues consider an ex-teen idol the kiss of death."

"Thank you for inviting me along. I would have never done anything like this on my own."

"The shows wouldn't have been half as good without you."

"And I helped you find the killer," she said.

"I'm better at solving mysteries than you give me credit."

"Okay, when we get home, I challenge you to a jigsaw competition."

"You're on," I said. "So what are you going to do with your share of the reward money?"

"I want to find a new place to live. Some place quiet and safe. If I have enough money left over, I want to get a piano and start playing again."

"Why don't you take the keyboard I have?" I said.

"I couldn't."

"Go ahead. I don't use it much. If I ever start recording again, I can get another one."

"Thanks."

"And that's not all you're getting. I'm using some of my reward money to buy you a dog."

"Ernest, I can't take care of a pet."

"I'm not talking about a pet. It's a guide dog so you can get out of the house."

"A guide dog! How wonderful!" Celeste hugged me. She tried to kiss my cheek and ended up smooching my ear instead. I didn't mind. After all the years of animosity between us, I was just happy to see Celeste in good spirits.

"Ernest, remember what Madame Balorinsky said about someone new coming into my life? Maybe she meant the guide dog!"

"Don't be silly. Those predictions are so vague that they

could mean anything."

"You're such a cynic."

"And you're such a dreamer."

Back in L.A., I dropped off Celeste at her house. In my home, I dumped the suitcases on the floor to tend to later and checked my answering machine. Only two of the calls interested me. Marshall said Rhino Records was making a CD compilation set of obscure '70s folk rock artists and was interested in using my sister's songs. What a nice break for Celeste. But Marshall had no jobs for me, the bum.

The other call was from my mother. She said the expected financing from the potential donors had failed to come through. My father was going to lose his beloved orchestra.

THE END

TEEN IDOL QUIZ

A true fan knows everything about her idol along with his family and friends! See how much you love Sandy Fairfax, star of the smash '70s TV show, *Buddy Brave, Boy Sleuth*. All the answers can be found in *The Cunning Cruise Ship Caper*.

1. During a concert, Sandy tap dances or soft shoe shuffles during what song?

2. What are the names of the two albums Celeste recorded in the 1970s?

3. On which *Buddy Brave* episode did Sandy dress up as Robin Hood?

4. What is the name of Cinnamon Lovett's dance school?

5. What is Sandy's birth date and zodiac sign?

6. How many bedrooms are in Sandy's house?

7. What studio did Sandy use to record his 1970s albums?

8. In what city does Sandy's A.A. group meet?

9. What instrument does Celeste play?

10. What is Sandy going to buy for his sister with his share of the reward money?

Count up your correct answers. How well did you score?

0 to 2—Man overboard
3 to 5—Stowaway
6 to 8—First mate
9 to 10—Captain

QUIZ ANSWERS

1. *Top Hat and Tails*
2. *A Dragon in the Forest* and *Gently Sings the Dove*
3. "The Shady Sherwood Forest Caper"
4. Dance Delight Studio
5. December 25, 1955. He's a Capricorn.
6. Four
7. Capital Records in Hollywood
8. Beverly Hills
9. Piano/keyboards
10. A guide dog for the blind

Sandy Fairfax Discography

All records except *Sessions* and *Black Wave* originally released on the SuperTonic label

Sincerely Yours, Sandy. "Girl of My Dreams"/"Spark of Love" 1975

Soda Shoppe. "Cuddle Close"/"Sweet as Can Be" 1976

Walk in the Park. "Weeping Willow"/"Every Jack Has His Jill" 1976

Stars in My Eyes. "Little Bunny Bright Eyes"/"Didn't I See You Looking (at Another Boy)" 1977

Dancin' Sandy. "Meet Me at the Disco"/"Swing to the Beat" 1977

Sandy Sings Live For You (concert album) 1977

Knight in Shining Armor. "Tell Me True (I Love You)"/"Tomboy in Pink Ribbons" 1978

Sandy Rings in the Holidays. "Mistletoe Kiss"/"Sugar Plums and You" 1978

Castles in the Air. "Moonbeam Melinda"/"The Picture in the Locket" 1979

Sandy's Tastiest Treats (greatest hits) 1980

Peanut Butter and Jam Sessions (independent label) 1985

Black Wave (with the band Shipwreck) 1988

Movies And Television

Buddy Brave, Boy Sleuth (live action TV series) 1975-1979

Buddy Brave And The Suspicious Spy (movie) 1975

Buddy Brave And the Dangerous Demon (movie) 1976

The Secret Files Of Buddy Brave (animated TV series) 1979-1980

Charlie's Angels (guest appearance) 1980

Fantasy Island (guest appearance) 1983

The Love Boat (guest appearance) 1985

Off-Kelter (guest appearance) 1993

ABOUT THE AUTHOR

 Sally Carpenter is a native Hoosier now living in Moorpark, California. She has a master's degree in theater from Indiana State University. While in school, her plays *Star Collector* and *Common Ground* were finalists in the American College Theater Festival One-Act Playwriting Competition. *Common Ground* also earned a college creative writing award. *Star Collector* was produced in New York City and was also the inspiration for her book series.

Carpenter also has a master's degree in theology and a black belt in tae kwon do. She's worked as an actress, college writing instructor, theater critic, jail chaplain and tour guide/page for Paramount Pictures. She's now employed at a community newspaper.

Her first book in the Sandy Fairfax Teen Idol mystery series, *The Baffled Beatlemaniac Caper*, was a 2012 *Eureka!* Award finalist for best first mystery novel. The second book *The Sinister Sitcom Caper*, is published by Cozy Cat Press.

Her short story, "Dark Nights at the Deluxe Drive-in," is in the anthology, *Last Exit to Murder*. "Faster Than a Speeding Bullet" can be found in the *Plan B: Vol. 2* e-book anthology.

She's a member of Sisters in Crime/Los Angeles. She's also "mom" to two black cats. Contact her on Facebook or scwriter@earthlink.net. She blogs at http://sandyfairfaxauthor.com.